UNDRESSING THE DUKE

LORDS IN LOVE #7

ERICA RIDLEY

Copyright © 2022 Erica Ridley

Original anthology: *Duke in a Box*

All rights reserved.

This is a work of fiction. Names, characters, places, and incidents are the product of the author's imagination or are used fictitiously. Any resemblance to actual events, locales, or persons, living or dead, is purely coincidental.

Cover design © Dar Albert

ALSO BY ERICA RIDLEY

The *Dukes of War*:
The Viscount's Tempting Minx
The Earl's Defiant Wallflower
The Captain's Bluestocking Mistress
The Major's Faux Fiancée
The Brigadier's Runaway Bride
The Pirate's Tempting Stowaway
The Duke's Accidental Wife
A Match, Unmasked
All I Want

The *Wild Wynchesters*:
The Governess Gambit
The Duke Heist
The Perks of Loving a Wallflower
Nobody's Princess
My Rogue to Ruin

Heist Club:
The Rake Mistake
The Modiste Mishap

Rogues to Riches:
Lord of Chance

Lord of Pleasure
Lord of Night
Lord of Temptation
Lord of Secrets
Lord of Vice
Lord of the Masquerade

The *12 Dukes of Christmas*:
Once Upon a Duke
Kiss of a Duke
Wish Upon a Duke
Never Say Duke
Dukes, Actually
The Duke's Bride
The Duke's Embrace
The Duke's Desire
Dawn With a Duke
One Night With a Duke
Ten Days With a Duke
Forever Your Duke
Making Merry

***Gothic Love Stories*:**
Too Wicked to Kiss
Too Sinful to Deny
Too Tempting to Resist
Too Wanton to Wed
Too Brazen to Bite

Magic & Mayhem:

Kissed by Magic

Must Love Magic

Smitten by Magic

Regency Fairy Tales

Bianca & the Huntsman

Her Princess at Midnight

Missing an Erica Ridley book?

Grab the latest edition of the free, downloadable and printable complete book list by series here:

https://ridley.vip/booklist

UNDRESSING THE DUKE

LORDS IN LOVE #7

ACKNOWLEDGMENTS

As always, I could not have written this book without the invaluable support of many others. Huge thanks go out to Darcy Burke, Elyssa Patrick and Erica Monroe. You are the best!

I also want to thank my wonderful VIP readers, our Historical Romance Book Club on Facebook, and my fabulous early reader team. Your enthusiasm makes the romance happen.

Thank you so much!

ACKNOWLEDGMENTS

As always, I could not have written this book without the invaluable support of many others. Huge thanks go out to Darcy Burke, Elyssa Patrick and Erica Monroe. You are the best!

I also want to thank my wonderful VIP readers, our Historical Romance Book Club on Facebook, and my fabulous early reader team. Your enthusiasm makes the romance happen.

Thank you so much!

CHAPTER 1

*D*onovan Sutcliffe, the fifth duke of Southbury, stood in the center of a large private chamber with his patrician nose high in the air.

Most of his peers would opine that the duke always commanded a position of power in order to glower down his nose disapprovingly at the milling masses surrounding him. At the moment the audience was smaller, but just as demanding:

Donovan was alone in his dressing room with his valet Geoffrey, who was in the process of tying the duke's freshly starched cravat.

"Now, remember," Geoffrey said sternly, as he worked his magic. "Tonight at your mother's ball, we are debuting a delicate new waterfall of folds that are certain to take the cravat-wearing world by storm. I shall expire in a puddle of pure mortification if you mash my creation to bits with that strong, jutting chin of yours."

"I never lower my chin," the duke responded without irony.

Donovan indeed glared at his surroundings in silent imperiousness any time he was forced to mingle with the grasping sycophants and desperate debutantes of the ton.

These unfortunates assumed the duke's dour grimace to be a reflection of his intense distaste for those around him. Although a not entirely inaccurate assumption, as before, the truth was much simpler:

Donovan would sooner perish than disrupt a single crease of his valet's labor.

"Hold still," Geoffrey chided, though the duke had not moved a muscle.

By all accounts, Donovan was considered abnormally tall and improbably burly for a peer of the realm. Nonetheless, his French valet outperformed him in both these measures.

Geoffrey Vachon was six foot five, and bore the bulging muscles of a woodsy brute who regularly wrestled bears for a living. In fact, if one were feeling uncharitable in one's description, Geoffrey very much resembled a bear himself. Abominably tall, broad shoulders, hulking muscles. His shaggy, chocolatey-brown hair always curled away from his sculpted face in an exquisitely careless, flyaway manner belying the long hours necessary to achieve a look of such casual deshabille.

If one *were* feeling charitable—which Donovan was not; he never was—his grace would be forced to admit that the fussy hair and dandy-approved wardrobe stretching over the French valet's overlarge everything all summed up into one unreasonably attractive package.

6

It was a very good thing that the duke's valet would remain sequestered upstairs in Donovan's bedchambers rather than join the imminent festivities below, or the bachelor duke might find every female eye trained on his handsome valet instead of the unwed duke prowling in their midst.

"Your mother expects you to select a bride tonight," Geoffrey murmured, as if Donovan needed any such reminder.

The soon-to-be dowager duchess of Southbury was relentless in this desire.

The onslaught had begun the summer of Donovan's sixteenth year—the same year he had acquired Geoffrey. The valet, being French and three years Donovan's senior, had at the time seemed the most exotic and sophisticated creature on the planet.

Little had changed from that first impression, save to add *insufferably impertinent* to the list. Much like his mother.

Her grace's attempts to marry off her eldest son had begun in a predictable manner. Exhortations to dance with every heiress and wallflower alike. Endless supper parties and teas and assemblies and picnics.

In the twenty years since, his mother's efforts had redoubled in line with her desperation.

"I don't perceive a reason to hurry," Donovan grumbled.

At the advanced age of six-and-thirty, he was perhaps no longer *young*—at least, not in the eyes of fresh-faced sixteen-year-old debutantes—but hunched and wrinkly peers of twice Donovan's age regularly snapped up nubile young brides, despite their clumsy arthritic hands and the overgrown bushes of white hairs protruding from their droopy ears. The duke was not in dire straits.

Besides, Mother had already achieved one resounding success: Donovan's younger brother Bernard had met and married his bride over a decade ago. Together, they'd spawned not one but *three* strapping young sons.

One might think such an achievement would make her grace happy.

Instead, it merely gave Mother more ammunition to use against Donovan. If he heard *Why can't you be as romantic as your brother?* one more bloody time...

"Are you going to dance tonight?" Geoffrey asked, as he stepped back to peer critically at his frothy creation.

"No," Donovan said with a sniff. "I never do."

That was the difference between being the heir apparent and being the duke. As a lad, he had been forced to follow his parents' dictates, and dance until dawn regardless of his own desires.

As duke, he need only provide his presence. No dancing. No flirting. No fuss.

His valet sent him a provocative look. "I've heard dancing can be fun, Adonis."

"That is not my name," Donovan replied tersely.

"It ought to be," Geoffrey parried back, as he always did. "You're built like a Greek statue and you comport yourself like one, too."

8

"You said to hold still," Donovan growled. "Does my cravat meet your approval or not?"

Geoffrey produced a pair of spectacles and made a slow production out of peering up and down Donovan's form at length, before bursting out laughing.

Donovan glared at him.

"Oh, you're a fine package and you know it." The valet dropped the spectacles back into his coat pocket with a chuckle. "And you hardly need *my* help to be starchy and buttoned-up."

"What about my shave?" Donovan asked. "Did the razor cut close enough this morning, or should we—"

Geoffrey's warm fingers softly cupped the side of Donovan's head. The valet lightly rubbed the pad of his thumb against the line of Donovan's jaw to test for stubble.

This, too, was part of their routine. Before exiting his dressing chamber, the duke questioned every aspect of Geoffrey's labor—upon which the valet ran his strong hands over every crease and seam in order to ensure not a single stitch was out of place.

"Your face is perfect," Geoffrey said softly. "As is the rest of your strapping self."

Donovan harrumphed. "Bollocks. You have to say that. I pay your salary."

The valet lowered his hand to his hip. "I would wager that same salary that every woman in the ballroom tonight will have the very same thought when she claps eyes on you: *What a fine and handsome duke.*"

"More like, *What a rude, condescending bore,*" Donovan corrected him.

"Only because you choose to be," Geoffrey chided him. The valet tucked his hands behind his back. "I've heard that all of the most celebrated beauties will be in attendance tonight. The angelic Miss Bromfield, the delectable Lady Cassandra, both of the buxom Musgrave twins…"

"And how do *you* know which nymphs of the beau monde are the prettiest, much less in possession of an invitation?"

Geoffrey scoffed lightly. "Do you think *anything* happens in this house without the servants' full awareness?"

"No." Donovan was very much aware that all the wealth and privilege in the world did not buy him a single ounce of privacy. The invisible eyes and ears of omnipresent members of staff arguably informed the duke's actions and legendary self-control far more than any edict from his parents or his peers.

"Consider speaking to someone tonight," said Geoffrey. "The evening might be more enjoyable if you don't spend it entirely stern and silent."

"There's no one I care to speak to," Donovan said bluntly.

"You talk to me," Geoffrey pointed out.

"And perhaps if you were a debutante in frilly lace…" Appalled, the duke cut off his words with a choking sound, the back of his neck flaming with heat beneath his expertly tied cravat. "I meant…"

Geoffrey held his gaze. "I know what you meant."

"Do you?" Donovan muttered, as he elbowed past his valet rudely instead of stepping politely around. "I have to go. Mother is waiting."

"My best regards to her grace."

Donovan rolled his eyes. "Mother hasn't noticed a servant in fifty years."

"Tell her anyway. For my own amusement."

"Very well." Donovan opened the dressing-room door and paused to glance back over his shoulder.

Geoffrey was still standing where Donovan had left him, hands behind his back, a small smile above his cleft chin, brown hair soft and tousled, looking every inch a proper dandy, and not at all like an overworked servant about to receive six hours' reprieve from his master.

"Stop twisting about," Geoffrey said softly. "Your powerful neck will crease my handiwork and we'll have to start the process all over again."

At this, Donovan was tempted to give an exaggerated nod and begin anew. Instead, he turned and stalked across the corridor and down the stairs to the cursed receiving line in the gilded salon. He'd have to stand at his mother's elbow for the next hour, greeting each unwanted guest as they invaded his home.

"*There* you are," scolded his mother upon sight of him. "At least you look presentable, as always. Tonight, can you *please* try to select a woman you can stand at least a little bit? And then make her your wife?"

He glared down his nose at her in disapproving silence.

She carried on, undaunted. "As soon as you take a bride, I can cease these infernal parties and spare us both. Dragging your feet only prolongs the torture."

"Are you under the mistaken impression that whomever I choose as my future duchess is likely to *refrain* from entertaining guests?"

"At least she won't be after you to hunt another bride," Mother replied unrepentantly. "You'll be free to glower unbecomingly in stony silence for the rest of your life."

He grunted. "I'm free to do so now. Geoffrey sends his love, by the way."

She stared at him. "Who the devil is Geoffrey? Would you *please* pay a modicum of attention to the problem at hand? Tonight we shall have in attendance four diamonds of the first water. The first girl who could make you a suitable bride is the lovely—"

The duke ceased listening. He'd already heard more than enough about angelic blonds and buxom twins from Geoffrey, who paid attention to such things.

Donovan had *tried* to. He'd spent every year of his time at Eton and Cambridge willing himself to give a damn about carousing and wenching, all without success.

He was not a complete buffoon. Donovan registered women's relative attractiveness just as he noticed a pretty landscape or the cuteness of a baby duckling. Though he wouldn't wish to leg-shackle himself to one of those, either.

"Announcing tonight's first guests!" the butler's voice rang out, interrupting the duchess's lecture.

"Thank God," Donovan muttered.

"Lord and Lady Bernard Sutcliffe!" boomed the butler.

The elegant couple swept into the ballroom smiling ear-to-ear, as was their wont. Unlike the duke, his brother Bernard and sister-in-law Sorcha adored functions such as this one, and would likely dance every set, including a scandalous number of waltzes with each other.

They hurried up to Donovan and the duchess to exchange pleasantries and air-kisses.

Whilst Sorcha gabbed animatedly with Donovan's mother, his brother grabbed the duke by the shoulders. "I have marvelous news!"

Donovan doubted this immensely, and stiffened with trepidation. "Don't wrinkle my sleeves. Just tell me."

"As you may recall, May Day marks the anniversary of when I first laid eyes on my future bride."

How could Donovan not recall? Bernard not only waxed on about this happy accident at length every time he imbibed an inch of port, but the romantic fool also hied off with his wife in tow every spring like clockwork, to spend a nostalgic week at the same May Day festival in a day's drive away in Marrywell, where he and Sorcha had first met.

"It's known as a matchmaking holiday for a reason," Bernard said as he dug a conspiratorial elbow into Donovan's perfectly tailored ribs.

13

"Anyone suffering from an uninspiring season need only visit Marrywell during the May Day fertility festival in order to find themselves tumbling arse over teakettle in love."

"As you and Sorcha did," Donovan interrupted, in an attempt to hurry the worn-out story along.

"As *you* will as well, big brother," Bernard crowed.

Donovan froze. "What?"

"Sorcha and I will bring you along on this year's pilgrimage. We'll have an absolutely stupendous time."

"I shan't go."

"No, of course you shan't," Bernard agreed. "Not if you choose a bride at *tonight's* ball. But in the... dare I say, *exceedingly* likely event... that none of the succulent sweets on display tempt your palate, there will be no choice but to fish in an alternate pond. As they say, if the mountain will not come to the Duke of Southbury..."

"You're mixing your metaphors," Donovan said dourly.

"And you, old chap, will soon be packing your bags," Bernard replied cheerfully. "Or having your valet do it."

"I won't go," the duke repeated.

"You have to." His younger brother made an apologetic grimace, then played his trump card. "I've already promised Mother."

CHAPTER 2

*A*fter the final guest departed at a quarter past four in the morning, Donovan escorted his mother to her guest quarters, then trudged toward his bedchamber with aching feet.

Not only had he failed to select a bride and thereby escape his impending forced holiday to Marrywell's matchmaking festival, Donovan also hadn't danced a single set—or even exchanged more than a few words with any of the marriageable young ladies present.

At six-and-thirty, what was a man supposed to say to a girl twenty years his junior? *Good evening, I'm old enough to be your father, what a drizzly day we're having, why yes that is a nice hair ribbon, how fortunate you must feel, shall I ring for tea?*

Consign himself to three or four *decades* of such scintillating conversation? Over Donovan's dead body.

Debutantes were wholly out of the question. Not that the spinsters were much better stock.

The duke had nothing against them, of course. He was the male version of a spinster. But he no more understood them than he did the debutantes.

Which left what... widows? Mother would be appalled if he passed over the season's sparkliest debutantes. But of all the options, it was perhaps the best one.

A widow would not look at him with the starry-eyed innocence of a debutante, or with the jaded resentment of a long-overlooked spinster. A widow had *had* her chance at love. Knew what she was getting with a marriage. Had tasted subsequent independence and likely longed for more of it—making her amenable to a union of convenience, in which duke and duchess did each other the blessed courtesy of leaving one another the hell alone.

Donovan pushed open the door to his bedchamber.

Geoffrey was still awake.

Instead of Donovan being greeted by shadowy blackness, choice candles were lit throughout the private apartment, lending a soft glow to his tired eyes rather than harsh light reflected in a dozen mirrors.

"You waited up for me," Donovan said unnecessarily.

Geoffrey smiled. "You pay my salary, remember?"

Donovan had no idea when Geoffrey managed to sleep, since he was always alert, attentive, and in impeccable attire any time Donovan glimpsed him.

He had spent their first years together begging in vain for Geoffrey to get some sleep whilst Donovan went about his duties, rather than wait up for an unknown amount of time, on the off chance the duke should return earlier than expected and require some sort of sartorial assistance.

Around the time the duke turned twenty-five —and his valet, twenty-eight—Donovan gave up on convincing the man to allow himself to take first priority once in a while, and instead gratefully accepted Geoffrey's company.

"Long day of dancing?" the valet enquired, his chiseled features beautiful in the candlelight.

"Long night of standing immobile, my spine ramrod straight and my nose in the air, allowing only the occasional flicker of my eyes to convey my utter and infinite disapproval."

Geoffrey clucked his tongue. "Ah, my surly Adonis. What *shall* I do with you?"

"Get me out of these clothes," Donovan commanded. "They reek of three dozen matchmaking mamas' undisguised despair."

"At once, your grace."

Another little jest. Whenever Geoffrey said *at once*, it almost certainly meant he was about to take his sweet time performing whatever task he had just promised to do.

Donovan held perfectly still as his handsome valet approached and began the slow, painstaking process of disarming the duke's cravat. Fold by fold. Crease by crease. Occasionally, Geoffrey's knuckles grazed Donovan's jawline ever so lightly.

The tiniest kiss of flesh against flesh. Barely there, barely noticeable.

Perhaps the brief contact wouldn't even happen at all, were it not for the bobbing of Donovan's Adam's apple and the visible leap of his pulse at the base of his newly exposed throat. Once the cravat was folded and set aside, it was time for Donovan's tail coat.

Geoffrey's long fingers could have made quick work of the buttons, but as usual, he took his time loosening each one, as though loath to place undue stress on a single strand of thread. Once the buttons were free, it was time to slide the ebony superfine from Donovan's shoulders.

It was not the duke's fault that the fashions of the day insisted a gentleman's wardrobe be tailored so close to his precise measurements that it was impossible to shrug in or out of one's coat without professional assistance.

The duke tried to hold still—truly, he did—but he might have accidentally flexed his arms ever so slightly when Geoffrey's hands skated over the muscles.

In no time, the duke's linen shirtsleeves billowed free. Geoffrey placed his palms on Donovan's chest and forced the duke backwards into a tall chair.

All right, *forced* might be a bit of a stretch. It was more like a waltz, with the duke obediently following his valet's lead. Donovan knew what was coming next. Had been dreaming of it during the entirety of his mother's insufferable ball.

Geoffrey sank to his knees before Donovan

and removed his dancing slippers one at a time, placing them to the side with his infernal careful precision. Then, and only then, did the valet lift his duke's stockinged foot into the valley of Geoffrey's closed thighs and begin to knead the tight muscles with his abnormally strong hands.

The first time his valet had attempted this maneuver, Donovan had objected vociferously. Somewhat vociferously. Very well: half-heartedly. He didn't know if others had ever attempted to dissuade someone from massaging one's sore muscles into such pure bliss that one very nearly purrs with pleasure, but it was not within the duke's power to resist for long.

Was this extended caress a valet's duty? Probably not. But then, when had Geoffrey ever cared about the limits of a valet's duty? It was unfair, abominable really, all the tasks that Geoffrey assumed that by rights ought to go to someone else —or to no one at all. He was more than a valet. He was a maid, a footman, a masseur. Any task that took place within Donovan's private chambers was performed by Geoffrey, or no one at all.

This one just happened to be one of the most pleasurable.

Donovan's head lolled back against the side wing of his tall chair. A whimper escaped his throat. He tried to recall the sound, but it was too late. The soft little moan of pleasure was out there, reverberating through the room, bouncing and refracting off every surface like a thousand beams of light.

He opened his eyes to see Geoffrey's hooded

brown eyes watching him with an unreadable gaze.

Their relationship was not strictly master-and-servant, which only served to confuse matters even more. On nights that did not require foot massages before a low fire, Donovan and his valet might be found playing cards until the wee hours of the morning, or hunched over Donovan's grandfather's chess board, at which it was difficult to tell which of the men had less aptitude for the game. It was not unusual for them to notice eight moves later that a pawn could have taken the king at any time.

Perhaps their questionable acuity could be blamed on the bottles of wine that usually accompanied such lazy evenings together. Or perhaps it was due to their long, rambling conversations, that began one place and ended up detouring through five others.

They had spent hours of every day together for so long, Geoffrey's presence was like the rising of the sun and moon, or the ebb and flow of the tides. Gentle. Dangerous. Captivating. The predictable rhythm potent and seductive, no matter how many times one stood on the shore and waded into the water.

"How does that feel?" Geoffrey murmured as he worked his thumbs into the duke's muscles.

"Good." The word rasped from Donovan's throat as it always did, hoarse and breathy. Barely audible, even in the dark stillness of the middle of the night.

A tiny smile teased the corners of Geoffrey's

wide lips. He knew exactly how divine his massages felt, damn the man. He bloody well knew the duke was putty in his hands, unable to do more than melt into his chair bonelessly as Geoffrey worked the muscles of each foot in his strong grip.

A knock sounded at the door. Geoffrey set Donovan's foot aside—to the duke's bitter disappointment—and rose to his feet to answer the call.

It was a bath, of course. Donovan had not seen his valet tug a bell pull to summon the pails of steaming water, but Geoffrey was like that. He had probably sensed Donovan's imminent arrival seconds before the duke's hand touched the doorknob, and placed the order then.

"This way, if you please." Geoffrey led the footmen to the dressing room, where a large clawfoot tub imported from the Netherlands rested behind a tall folding screen.

The footmen filled the basin with their pails of piping hot water, then took their leave.

Donovan and Geoffrey were alone again.

The valet hummed beneath his breath as he added salts and perfumed soap to the water, testing its temperature occasionally with the tip of his finger until he determined the bath was nearly ready.

He turned to Donovan with a lift of his eyebrows. "Now, then. Shall we?"

Technically, the duke could do this part himself. Unlike skin-tight buckskins, formal breeches were easy to peel off, and his cambric shirt was so loose it could fly away in a gust of wind.

The duke could also bathe himself, if need be.

He might not know his knight from his bishop, but he certainly grasped the function of soap and water.

This *was* part of a valet's duties, however, just as a lady's maid undressed and bathed her mistress. It would be far stranger for Donovan to allow Geoffrey to take over every other possible role, then balk at his valet performing such an ordinary, quotidian task.

Then again, politely declining would be far easier than the mental calisthenics required to keep his naked body from responding visibly to his valet's touch.

God help him, that was a line Donovan did not dare cross. Certain acts were prohibited. A duke might get away with murder, but his valet could face disastrous legal or social consequences.

Not that Donovan was thinking about the law when he looked at Geoffrey. Rather, his mind jumbled with memories of every other moment in which his valet had touched him, caressed him, smiled at him. Moments that would vanish like smoke if Donovan's secret desires were neither welcomed nor reciprocated.

And so he kept the secret. Again. As he had for twenty years. Gritting his teeth against the exquisite sensation of the man he could not help but yearn for running his burly hands over Donovan's bare skin, slippery with soap and water.

It was pleasure. It was pain. An unspeakable torment from which Donovan never wished to escape. Heaven and hell in a clawfoot tub. Exposed. Vulnerable. Terrified.

And painfully aroused.

CHAPTER 3

$\mathcal{T}$he next morning, Donovan sat in the same chair before the same desk in the same study where he had spent the same post-breakfast hours every day for the past decade. To-day, rather than concentrate on the chart of ac-counts before him, the duke's eyes blurred.

Donovan allowed the ledger to tumble to the desk. He placed his elbows on either side of the fallen journal and cradled the top of his head in his hands.

He wasn't happy. Had perhaps never *been* truly happy. He had come close, on any number of oc-casions, for a moment or two. Riding a fast horse across the vast land of his country estate. Kneeling on his brother's sitting room carpet to play hobby-horse with his nephews.

And, of course, countless moments with Geof-frey. The half-remembered nights of drunken card games until neither knew how many points he had earned. The pact they had made never to study the rules and strategy of chess, so that their meandering games were always as absurd and light-hearted as the time before.

Or how about that summer after Eton? Donovan had attended a musicale at which a dozen debutantes performed, and decided to take up an instrument himself. There was not a huge demand for solo performances by seventeen-year-old dukes, even beneath Donovan's own roof.

To date, the only regular audience member the duke had ever had, was his valet Geoffrey, who had good-naturedly agreed to practice the violin along with him. Side by side, they had painstakingly learned to tune their instruments and rosin their bows and eke out sounds that were not entirely painful. Eventually, they outgrew the duke's tutor and continued studying on their own. Donovan acquired sheet music from all over Europe. The men crafted duets of all their favorite songs.

It was in those moments when the duke had been closest to happy. But what kind of life was that? Secretly playing Vivaldi with one's valet in the confines of one's private sitting room?

Lusting after said valet, despite all the reasons such an attachment was forbidden?

As much as Donovan hated to admit it, his mother was right.

From the moment he left his leading strings, the duke had been aware that it was his duty to continue the ducal line with care and honor. That he must one day take a wife and beget heirs of his own, instructing them in matters of comportment and responsibility so that they too would be prepared when it came time to inherit or pass down the title.

He'd successfully avoided that part of his destiny for six-and-thirty years. He could not keep doing so indefinitely. If the gap in ages between himself and this season's crop of debutantes seemed insurmountable now, the chasm would only grow worse the longer he procrastinated his fate.

Yes, this idea of finding a tolerable, romantically disengaged widow was the least distasteful solution. The upcoming matchmaking festival was old-fashioned and perhaps a sign of desperation, but it was a viable last resort. Bernard had met his wife at just such a May Day gathering, had he not? As had countless other lords. Why not Donovan, too?

"Because you don't want a wife," he muttered.

True, but since when had that signified? He didn't *want* to balance accounts or attend his mother's parties or listen to droning speeches in the House of Lords. But it wasn't up to him. These tasks were part of the job. He was a duke, like it or not, and therefore had a duty to act like one.

Which meant there was another change in store. One Donovan had been dreading for twenty years. His throat tightened.

When it came time to welcome a wife... it would also be time to dismiss his valet.

Nausea roiled in his gut at the thought, as it always did. He could not imagine a life without Geoffrey. He was the first person Donovan saw every morning, the last voice he heard every night. His constant companion, year after year, day after day. Whose stalwart presence Donovan had never once tired of.

If anything, to be separated from Geoffrey by so much as a common wall was to crave his company viscerally. And to be reunited, bliss. If perhaps a qualified bliss. Donovan could be seated across from his valet at a gaming table, or naked in a bath willing his cock not to rise, or holding perfectly still whilst the handsome hulking Geoffrey fussed with the duke's collar or buttons or stubborn cowlick… and *pine* for him most dreadfully, despite there being nothing more substantial than linen separating Donovan's flesh from Geoffrey's own.

It was this infernal pining that could not be withstood. Donovan could not give his future wife the romantic love or sexual desire any spouse would crave, but he was not so vile a creature as to force her to live in a house where her husband actively lusted for another inhabitant, day in and day out. Donovan would be far from a perfect husband, but at the very least, he would not disrespect his wife or break his marital vows. He could promise that much.

The duke lowered his hands from his face and shoved his journals of accounts aside. He drew toward himself instead fresh parchment, and pen and ink. He might have dreaded this moment for twenty years, but he had practiced it an infinite number of times in his mind.

His plume flew across the page as he extolled Geoffrey's talents, character, and expertise. Never in the history of England had there existed a letter of recommendation so effusive and iron-clad as the ones Donovan crafted now. Geoffrey would not simply be able to walk out the front door straight into alternate employment. He would be able to work for the king himself, at a salary unheard of for a servant.

Once the letters were written, the duke sagged back against the chair to watch the ink dry. Identical sheets of parchment papered his desk like the tiles of a roof. He'd made far more copies than Geoffrey could possibly use. More copies than existed peers of the realm.

But the duke would do nothing to jeopardize Geoffrey's future, even if Donovan could not be part of it himself.

When the ink was dry, the duke could not put off his abominable task any longer.

He gathered the letters into a tall stack, and encased them safely in a pristine leather satchel he had purchased for just this purpose.

In an hour, it would be time for tea. Geoffrey would be awaiting him in the private sitting room that had long since begun to feel like *theirs* rather than *Donovan's*.

But there would be no more teas. Not today or ever again.

He rang the bell-pull. A ridiculous series of events would now fall into motion. The cord traveled along the walls and down two floors to a corridor of bells just outside the scullery. A maid assigned to monitor for summons would alert one of her colleagues, who would race up two flights of stairs, normally to send a footman in to see the master. But Geoffrey had insisted long ago on being the one to interrupt Donovan, when such interruptions were necessary. So the maid would alert the valet, rather than a footman, and seconds later—

The door to Donovan's study swung open. Geoffrey was so tall and so wide as to fill every inch of the wooden frame. Donovan drank him in, unable to bear the realization that this would be the last time he would ever be able to do so.

At some unknown flicker behind Donovan's pained eyes, Geoffrey's easy smile faltered, and his warm expression turned to one of confusion, then alarm.

He strode forward quickly. "Is something wrong?"

Yes. Everything.

He lusted after his valet. It was inaccurate to call Geoffrey a temptation. Temptation implied a desire for something one could reach out and have. Geoffrey was torture. Donovan could not look at him without wanting him. Could not hear his voice without wanting him. Could not smell his cologne without wanting him. Could not feel his touch without wanting to rip his own clothes off and Geoffrey's, too.

And after surviving all these years of torment, Donovan still didn't know how Geoffrey felt about men who liked other men. What if Donovan hinted at the subject, only for Geoffrey to recoil in disgust or censure? Even if Geoffrey shared the same tendency, that did not mean he wished for an affair with Donovan in specific. Either way spelled rejection and heartache. Not that society would allow them to be together, anyway.

Every shared moment of the day was agonizing, and Donovan was tired of being miserable. Enough was enough. He would withstand this torment no longer. Society expected dukes to marry well and beget heirs. Geoffrey must expect it, too. The time had come to say goodbye.

Donovan scooped up the leather parcel and rose to his feet. "I need to speak with you about something important."

"Of course. Should I take a seat?"

"That won't be necessary." The duke cleared his suddenly tight throat. "I fear I must ask you to take an action you are not expecting to perform."

"It is my honor," Geoffrey answered without hesitation. "I am yours to command, now and always."

"Not always. Not anymore." Donovan held out the leather satchel.

Geoffrey did not take it. "What is that?"

"Yours, now. It contains one hundred letters of recommendation."

"One hundred..." Geoffrey's brown eyes filled with sudden understanding—and pain. "Recommending me for what?"

His strong voice broke on the last syllable, rendering the word *what* a nearly unintelligible croak.

Not that the question was necessary. They were now both going through the motions of a play that had been scripted against their will.

"The position of valet," Donovan said briskly,

as if this conversation were not rending his heart in two. "With the words I have written here, Brummell himself would salivate to have a single second of your time. Prinny would hire you in a heartbeat. The world is yours."

"The world is mine," Geoffrey repeated quietly. "But not the... *post* that I have loved for twenty years."

"You have done nothing wrong," Donovan said quickly. "You are exemplary in every way, and by every measure."

Geoffrey's eyes were anguished. "Then why—"

"*I cannot*," the duke burst out, his voice and fingers shaking. "I cannot continue as I have been, clinging to a path that goes nowhere. Tomorrow I leave with my brother and his wife for a May Day celebration, at which I shall select a wife."

Geoffrey stared at him as though the words held no meaning. "A wife."

"A future duchess," Donovan explained, "who deserves and shall receive one hundred percent of her husband's attention and respect."

This would solve all of his problems. He would not be the first peer to enter a loveless marriage, nor the last. It was a traditional path, and for Donovan, the only path. He might not be enthusiastic about selecting a bride, but the duke was faithful and loyal. From the moment he placed the ring on her finger, Donovan would not stray. Attraction to others would be irrelevant. There would be no more questions, no more wondering, no more waiting for a sign that would never come. A future that could never be.

"I am not the boy you met all those years ago, but a grown man," Donovan said briskly. "Being bosom friends with one's valet might be marginally more acceptable for a lonely lad in boarding school, but those days are gone. I am done raising eyebrows. I must sever ties so that I can marry a woman of my own class and undertake a normal, respectable, ducal life."

Geoffrey made no response, save to gaze at the duke with hurt, accusing eyes.

Donovan pretended not to notice. He proffered the satchel again instead. "Take it."

Geoffrey took it as though the bag contained a live bomb about to explode his life into a thousand pieces.

"Of course you must have a wife," the valet murmured, his face pale. "I've always known... I just didn't think... She... You and I..." He swallowed visibly. "You wrote letters of recommendation. I suppose I should thank you."

Donovan had never felt more of a wretch in his life.

He gripped the edge of the desk for support. "The last thing I wish to do is dismiss you."

"Then why must I—"

"Because 'duke' is not a post *I* can walk away from. I'm sorry, Geoffrey. Believe me when I say that every minute in your company has been..." Donovan could not continue. There were no words capable of explaining the emotion trapped in his chest. "Goodbye, old friend. I will miss you."

Geoffrey blinked. "It's to be immediate, then? No fortnight's notice?"

"You'll find a full year's compensation inside that satchel."

"I see." Geoffrey rolled back his broad shoulders. "You are generous to a fault, my lord."

You are worth that and more, the duke responded only in his head.

Geoffrey nodded once, then turned toward the door. "I'll be gone within a quarter hour."

Donovan watched him leave. His hands still gripped the side of his desk to prevent himself from reaching for the leather satchel and flinging it aside, then yanking his valet into his arms and crushing his firm lips with a kiss.

It was better to leave things like this. Cold. Professional.

Final.

When the door clicked into place, Donovan sank back into his chair. If his columns of accounts had blurred before, there was no hope of making sense of them now.

Not when it felt as though the satchel itself was a grenade. Once which had gone off without warning, exploding through Donovan's chest and shattering him into a thousand tiny shards.

With growing agony, he watched the minute hand on his tall case clock tick forward. Five minutes. Ten. Fifteen.

Geoffrey was a man of his word. He had left by now.

Gone.

Forever.

"*God damn it.*" Donovan swiped his arm across

his desk, knocking all of his ducal responsibilities to the floor.

In most aristocratic households, a lord in possession of a household of servants would barely have time to hear fallen objects clatter before maids and footmen rushed in to tidy his mess. In Donovan's home, it was always Geoffrey who hovered a heartbeat away, ready to step forward at the slightest sign he might be needed.

He wasn't here now, and would never be again. Those days were done. The clock marched on.

The question was whether *Donovan* could go on. One day, yes, he would be forced to take up the full mantle of his title and all the matrimonial responsibilities it entailed, but today need not be that day. If he acted quickly, he might still manage a short reprieve.

Donovan sprang up from his chair and bolted from the study. Heart pounding, lungs panting, he raced through the corridor and down the stairs and past the startled butler and out the front door and onto the garden.

A hackney carriage was just pulling to a stop next to Geoffrey and a single tall valise.

"Wait!" Donovan shouted, the word tangling in his throat and getting whipped by the wind, yet somehow reaching Geoffrey's ears.

His valet spun about, hope and wariness competing in his eyes.

"You're right," Donovan called out. "You deserve a fortnight's notice. It's only fair. I was hasty. I wasn't thinking... I didn't realize I wouldn't be able… A year's severance isn't enough. I'll fix that, too. Just… Come back. Come *with* me."

Geoffrey blinked. "Go with you where?"

"To Marrywell," Donovan answered. "Where even dukes fall in love."

CHAPTER 4

The following morning, Donovan and his not-entirely-dismissed valet set out for Marrywell in the ducal coach-and-four. Ten yards ahead, a similar black carriage contained his brother Bernard and sister-in-law Sorcha.

They had invited Donovan to join them, and to send along any necessary attendants in one of the two trailing carriages containing trunks and servants. The duke had declined as politely as he was able. Making this pilgrimage was concession enough. Suffering through two blissful lovebirds chirping on about all the beautiful women Donovan would soon be surrounded by, and the imminent date in which he would be leg-shackled to one for the rest of his life…

Good God, no. He'd rather *walk* the sixty miles than pretend to smile for eight hours at the prospect of a future so bleak.

Not to mention… Eight hours in a private cabin with Geoffrey was not a treat the duke was willing to deny himself.

Just *looking* at his valet was a balm to Donovan's soul. They were seated across from each other, Donovan facing forward and his valet facing the rear. Geoffrey's bulky shoulders and ridiculous height made the cavernous carriage feel cozy and intimate. The windows were unobstructed, but thus far the men only had eyes for each other.

Proper posture had flown out the door, and both men leaned back with their legs sprawling forward casually. Both had opted for pantaloons, which meant the form-fitting material stretched across their large, muscular legs. Because of the limited space, their limbs had no choice but to intertwine.

Donovan tried his best to pretend disinterest in the firm muscles of his valet's log-sized legs, or in how Geoffrey's thick arms and muscled chest might look if they were not hidden by layers of cambric and superfine.

He scrambled for the deck of cards hidden in his traveling bag instead. "Shall we play cards to pass the time?"

Geoffrey arched an amused brown brow. "Bored already, your grace?"

Anything but bored. Donovan could happily stare at Geoffrey's leg muscles and speculate about the rest of his form for the entire journey.

But he was resolved to fulfill the responsibilities of his title. Which meant choosing a wife, not lusting after his staff.

Or in this case, after Geoffrey's staff.

"We left the last game at a tie," the duke said

briskly, as though that were the cause of the thick tension inside the moving carriage.

"God forbid I should leave my post as your equal in any way," Geoffrey murmured.

Donovan looked at him sharply. Though it was true that the duke tended to win at Casino... Though it was also true that Donovan was the employer and Geoffrey the mere servant... Though it was true that dukes outranked every Englishman save the royal family...

Damn it all, he was not attempting to exert dominance in some playing-card fueled display of power!

"Forget the cards," Donovan said, tossing the unopened deck aside.

"What else do you have in there?" Geoffrey teased. "Lemonade? Watercolors?"

"A gag," the duke replied coldly.

Rather than cower with chagrin, his valet leaned forward with interest. "Can I see it?"

Donovan tossed his bag at him.

Geoffrey caught it easily and sorted through its contents with comical horror. "Carrots and oranges, rather than sweetmeats? Three flasks of tea, rather than whiskey? An almanac and your ledger to balance, rather than a torrid gothic novel to read?"

"I have my duty to consider," the duke bit out. "I told you."

Geoffrey snorted and tossed the bag back. "Have you never considered considering something else?"

Donovan fought the urge to cross his arms de-

fensively. "What could be more important than
duty?"

"*You* are," Geoffrey answered, his brown eyes
locking on the duke with surprising intensity.
"Trust me, I do understand that no matter what
you do, you will always be a duke, with all the responsibilities and pressures that title entails. But
you are also a person. A *man*. You are more than a
means to fulfill an obligation you never asked for."

"You make the privilege of peerage sound
horrid."

"Isn't it?" Geoffrey asked softly. "For you?"

Donovan glared back at him without responding.

Yes, damn it all, the privilege of peerage was the
worst punishment God could have devised for a
man only interested in other men. Not even Other
Men, plural. One man. Geoffrey Vachon, the big
infuriating hunk of handsome insolence seated
across from Donovan in the carriage.

"Promise me something," Geoffrey said.

"No," Donovan answered flatly.

Geoffrey carried on as if this interruption had
not occurred. "Promise me you'll at least *try* to
treat this holiday like a holiday."

"It is not a holiday." Marrywell was a prison
sentence. "This is a business errand to select an
appropriate bride."

"We both know you're not going to do that any
sooner than you absolutely have to. You'll pick a
chit at random at the last hour of the last day, and
then you'll regret that decision—whatever it is—
for the rest of your life."

"Thank you," Donovan said coldly. "That sounds charming."

"It sounds," Geoffrey corrected him, "like a full week of *no* responsibility, until the duty kicks in at the eleventh hour. I vote you treat it as such."

"You don't vote. This is not a democracy."

"It's seven days. *Seven.* Out of a lifetime of decades filled with nothing but duty. Would it really kill you to set responsibility aside for a single week?"

"This conversation is what's killing me. I am extinct. Please cease speaking."

"Forget about duty, then. Think about me."

"I never think about you," Donovan lied.

"You've given me my notice. We have one fortnight left together, before realistically never setting eyes on each other again. What if... you expended a hint of effort in an attempt to *enjoy* it?"

"I'm a duke. Peers don't expend effort. We have servants for that."

"If that were true, you wouldn't be hauling about a bag full of accounting journals and carrot sticks. I mean it, Southbury. Forget about duty for once, and have a week of just plain fun."

"What the devil is 'fun'?"

"God help us both." Geoffrey rolled his eyes toward the ceiling. "You need me even more than I feared."

Silence stretched between them.

"I know I do," the duke said gruffly. "Why else would I run after your carriage?"

Geoffrey's eyes locked with Donovan's. "I'm

glad you did, Southbury. No one else sees you like I see you."

Donovan's flesh heated in remembrance. Geoffrey had seen every inch of him, on countless occasions. The duke hadn't expected to ever be forced to *talk* about it.

"*I see you*," Geoffrey said, his gaze unflinching. "You are not the slab of marble you pretend to be."

"Isn't my statuesque demeanor why you call me Adonis?" the duke muttered.

"One reason," Geoffrey shot back.

Donovan lifted his nose and glared down at his valet imperiously. "I did not give you leave to call me 'Southbury.'"

"Did I?" Twin splotches of pink tinged his valet's sharp cheekbones. "I should not have done. Forgive me."

"Donovan," said the duke.

Geoffrey blinked owlishly. "I beg your pardon?"

"You may call me Donovan until you leave my household," the duke replied. "And I shall attempt to have 'fun' on this errand."

"Not an errand," Geoffrey reminded him. "The errand occurs on the last minute of the last hour. Between now and then is nothing but holiday. A full week of... anything you want."

The duke arched his brows with unmitigated skepticism. "*Anything* I want?"

"Anything," Geoffrey repeated softly. "*Donovan.*"

With those two words, the rest of the world disappeared. The clopping horses, the lumbering

41

carriage. Donovan did not feel like a buttoned-up duke in a traveling costume, but rather as vulnerable as he did kneeling naked before his valet in a basin of bathwater.

Donovan had never been more tempted to close the distance between them and haul his valet's beautiful lips against his own. He was always tempted. The past twenty years had been nothing but temptation. The exquisite torture of being touched by someone he did not dare touch back.

Yet, it had taken two decades and a dismissal for Donovan to give permission for Geoffrey to use his first name.

What would it take for him to reach across the carriage and run his hands over the hard planes of Geoffrey's chest, and broad shoulders, and strong arms, the way Donovan had long dreamed of doing? Five decades? Divine intervention?

The truth was, yearning was not enough. But making an explicit advance was not an overture one could walk back if it turned out to be unwanted.

It was not the sort of advance that should happen at all, and not only because they were both men. Such an unequal flirtation wouldn't be any more acceptable between a duke and his chambermaid. Donovan's desires were forbidden no matter which way he looked at them.

But he couldn't tear his gaze away. Not for the next eight hours. Not for the next seven days.

For as long as Geoffrey was still in sight, Donovan could at least daydream. Pretend that his desires were possible. That his years of pining in secret might culminate in more than the occasional tentative innuendo. That for once in his life, he could indeed have *fun*.

For as long as he had Geoffrey.

CHAPTER 5

$\mathcal{M}$arrywell. When Donovan's coach-and-four pulled to a stop in front of the inn hosting them for the week, his brother and sister-in-law were already exiting their carriage just before them. They hurried to greet Donovan's coach before the tiger even had the door open.

"What ho!" cried the ever-jovial Bernard as Donovan emerged from the carriage. "Did you enjoy your journey? Were you bored senseless without Sorcha and me to entertain you? Was the—Oh!"

Donovan turned to see what had caught his brother's eye.

It was Geoffrey, stepping down from the coach in all his sartorial glory. Six feet five inches and sixteen-and-a-half stone of solid muscle. Enormous feet clad in champagne-shined boots. Legs like tree trunks, encased in tight pantaloons. Trim hips beneath a sliver of glittering ruby-red waist-coat. Wide chest and impossible shoulders not just contained, but tailored into mouthwatering perfection. A strong jaw with the barest shadow. Chiseled cheekbones offset by meltingly warm brown eyes. Aggressively dark eyebrows barely visible beneath a fashionably shaggy mane of fly-away brown ringlets that begged to be touched.

At least, that was what Donovan saw. He imagined his brother was rather less discerning.

"I didn't know you were bringing a *friend*," Bernard exclaimed in raptures. "I didn't even know you *had* friends! Introduce me at once. I am charmed, I'm sure."

The duke and his valet exchanged a startled look at this comical misinterpretation of the scene at hand.

"He hasn't seen me in years," Geoffrey murmured.

And Bernard would not have paid much attention to his brother's valet, a decade ago when he still lived at home. Fashions had changed, Geoffrey had changed. His hair was different now, and there were new laugh lines at the corners of his eyes. Donovan supposed it was no wonder that Bernard would fail to recognize him.

The moment seemed to shimmer and sparkle with opportunity for mischief and adventure. Two words that had never before defined any aspect of Donovan's life or comportment.

But he had promised Geoffrey to take a true holiday this week, had he not? And as this comprised Donovan's final days to enjoy his valet's company, why not give Geoffrey some semblance of a holiday as well?

"Haven't you met?" Donovan asked his brother

45

with an expression he hoped implied innocent surprise. "Allow me to rectify this error at once. Bernard, my dear friend Mr. Geoffrey Vachon, whom I met during my time at Cambridge." This was true enough, though not in the way Bernard would assume. "Geoffrey, my brother and sister-in-law, Lord Bernard and Lady Sorcha."

Both Bernard and Sorcha beamed in obvious delight.

"The pleasure is surely mine," rumbled Geoffrey's low voice just behind Donovan's shoulder.

The duke did not dare turn around and meet his valet's eyes. He would either burst into child-like giggles if Geoffrey was half as amused at Donovan was... or turn cherry-red in mortification if his valet was less enthusiastic about the un-expected change in role.

"Have you a wife, Mr. Vachon?" Sorcha enquired.

"I do not," Geoffrey replied evenly.

She clapped her hands together. "Then before we leave, you will both surely find love!"

Donovan and Geoffrey carefully refrained from looking at each other.

"Come along," said Bernard, motioning them forward. "Let's sign the guest registry and beg for adjoining rooms."

Adjoining rooms.

A gentleman's valet often slept in a small chamber attached to his employer's dressing rooms. Although the actual connecting apartment intended for Donovan's future duchess had re-mained empty ever since he assumed the title, Geoffrey had never been more than a murmur away, even before Donovan had inherited the dukedom.

For the first time, however, Geoffrey would not be consigned to a dressing room or nearby servants' quarters, but rather, provided with an apartment very much the equal to the rooms rented to Donovan and Bernard.

"My apologies," the proprietor soon said to the group. "We are quite full. I can offer my largest chamber to the duke and his companion, but I'm afraid the room you and your wife have rented is located one floor above."

One room.

One.

Presumably with just one bed.

Sorcha made a commiserative expression. "Do you mind terribly, Southbury? We didn't know you would bring a friend, and the rooms in Marrywell fill months in advance. We can try another inn, but the fact of the matter is—"

"It's...fine," Donovan croaked. He hoped it was fine. He had not yet dared to glance at Geoffrey for confirmation.

"We should have requested adjoining rooms," Sorcha muttered.

"Well, if it's all the same to you, then it doesn't matter to us," said Bernard with his customary good cheer. "We may see you two when we break our fast, and perhaps attend some of the same activities."

Some of the same activities. Perhaps.

Donovan began to realize the enormity of what he'd done. His younger brother, who had long been convinced that he alone was his elder brother's social keeper, had taken Geoffrey's presence as a sign that Bernard was free to have a true holiday of his own. He could celebrate his anniversary with his wife at his leisure and pleasure, without any need to hover over a sibling whose legendary standoffishness had likely made Bernard despair of the duke even leaving his chamber.

The duke turned and met his valet's eyes.

Only someone who had known the man for as long as Donovan had would recognize the sparkle of impish amusement in Geoffrey's brown eyes.

"Mr. Vachon," said Donovan. "Would you be so kind as to instruct our respective servants on where to deliver our luggage?"

"Of course," Geoffrey murmured, and slipped off to explain the change in plans.

The footmen would not even blink. Not for the first time, Donovan was very grateful that his extremely well-paid staff could be trusted to keep the confidences of their eccentric master.

"He seems like a bang-up chap," said Bernard, and clapped the duke on the shoulder. "He'll keep you in line."

"And possibly be the first to find a wife," Sorcha teased. "You might hold a dukedom, but Mr. Vachon is very easy on the eyes."

"Oy!" Bernard clapped his hands to his chest and staggered as if struck by an arrow. "Have these twelve years together caused your eyes to wander?"

"Never!" Sorcha protested, wrapping her arms

about him. She cupped a hand to her mouth and stage-whispered to Donovan, "At least—not much."

"Grrr." Bernard rubbed his nose against his wife's and gave her a quick kiss. "When I get you into that bedchamber…"

She held up a finger, from which dangled a single brass key. "What are you waiting for?"

Bernard tossed Donovan a not-particularly-apologetic look. "You'll forgive me if my wife and I leave you and your friend to your own devices?"

"I shall manage," Donovan agreed magnanimously.

Bernard and Sorcha disappeared up the stairs as if in a puff of smoke.

Donovan shook his head fondly, an emotion he might not have experienced had he been forced to witness the lovebirds' endless amorous high jinks from an arm's length away for the entire holiday.

He turned from the staircase in time to see Geoffrey approaching.

"Message delivered," the valet murmured.

"I fear we shall not glimpse my brother and his wife again until the holiday concludes," Donovan informed him.

"Oh no," Geoffrey said with a blank face. "Whatever shall we do in their absence?"

"A wise man suggested I fill this week with something called 'fun,'" Donovan replied.

"It sounds decadent and dangerous," Geoffrey said. "We should have as much of it as possible."

CHAPTER 6

*D*onovan held up the key. "Shall we freshen up before heading out-of-doors?"

"Let's." Geoffrey gestured to indicate he would follow the duke.

Donovan strode toward their shared room with a mix of excitement and foreboding. Sharing sleeping quarters with the man he desired and could not have was going to be even more torment than he'd been forced to withstand thus far.

He unlocked the door. They stepped inside the apartment together. The entrance led to a small, but pretty parlor. Its cozy interior boasted a sofa, a pair of armchairs, and a tea table. That was innocuous enough. There was nothing at all untoward about two individuals enjoying a spot of tea.

The parlor connected to the other room. The bedchamber.

"Shall we?" his valet asked.

Donovan forced himself to lead the way. He nearly came to a dead stop in the doorway.

There was just one bed, exactly as he'd feared. And hoped. And feared. And hoped. And feared.

The bed was gratifying large, at least. Plenty of mattress space even for men the size of Donovan and Geoffrey to sleep in comfort without risk of bumping against each other in the night.

Sleep in comfort. Ha. Donovan had wanted to end the agony of emotions he could not act on, and instead the stakes were even higher. Willing his cock not to rise whilst being bathed was difficult enough. Hiding a morning erection would be all but impossible. Hiding an all-night-long cockstand...

"Well, this is awkward," Donovan muttered.

Geoffrey did not respond. If only Donovan knew what his valet was feeling! Revulsion? Interest? Dread?

"The sofa is too small for either of us to lie upon," Donovan said carefully. "We'll have to share the bed."

Geoffrey's expression was frustratingly blank. "Which side do you want?"

The bottom was unquestionably the wrong answer, so Donovan said, "I'll take the left."

"Then I'll take the right." Geoffrey sat on the edge of the mattress as though to test its thickness, then ran a hand over his pillow. "There's only one armoire, but there should be plenty of room for both our things."

Leave it to a valet to be more concerned about where to store the cravats than how to share the bed. Donovan didn't know whether to be relieved that the status quo between them had not been threatened, or if he should scream into a pillow.

That was his answer, then. Mahogany furniture interested Geoffrey more than any wood Donovan might provide. Good. That made things easier. Dismissing his valet had been the right move all along. Donovan had always known there was no future between them, but now there was no doubt. He could move on, just as he'd planned.

After he'd survived one last week of tortuous proximity.

No. He couldn't do it. He could not possibly share a bed with this man and be dressed by this man and be bathed by this man and still somehow manage to hide how he felt. Not when they were sharing a bedchamber.

There was nothing to do about the sleeping arrangements, but as to the rest...

"As far as anyone knows, you're here as my friend, not my servant," he began.

Geoffrey inclined his head. "I am both. Or at least I was, until you dismissed me."

That was the answer! Donovan's tight shoulders relaxed a fraction in relief. "Just so. Therefore, while we are here in Marrywell, you are to act as my friend, and not my valet. I shall attend to my own needs—"

Oh, God, *needs* was the wrong word. It made Donovan think of all the nights he'd wrapped his hand around his cock in furtive desperation to relieve the painful pressure building in his balls every time he thought of Geoffrey.

"By which I mean my attire," Donovan blurted

out. "And… and all related concerns. While we are here, you are not my valet. I shall manage myself."

He hoped. How hard could it be? It didn't matter. When they returned from Marrywell, Geoffrey would only be in Donovan's employ for a few days more. The duke would have to get on without his valet soon enough. He might as well start now. The experiment might even make him all the more appreciative of the new, hideous-but-capable valet he'd be hiring to replace the current one.

Geoffrey shrugged. "As you wish."

There. That was settled. Having rules to govern the next week and define their roles made Donovan happy. He liked knowing where the lines were, so that he could stay within them…and out of trouble.

He'd spent years avoiding social situations when possible, and comporting himself appropriately when they could not be avoided. Just like he'd spent years tamping down his inconvenient feelings for his valet. He knew how he was expected to behave, and did his best to act accordingly.

Donovan abhorred change of any sort. He'd been born with the forewarning that taking a bride would one day alter his life, but he had not been prepared for *this*. Sharing a bedchamber with Geoffrey was more than a mere disruption to the ordinary. Donovan would have to do everything in his power to limit their time together in this room to the hours in which both were fast asleep.

It was a good thing there was a festival taking

place right outside these walls. It was the perfect distraction.

Even if it meant willingly submerging himself in social interaction.

A knock sounded on the door. Geoffrey glanced at Donovan. "Shall I?"

"Please."

Their valises had arrived. Donovan watched in silence as his valet unpacked his own valise first, only to recall once Geoffrey finished and wandered back to the parlor to inspect the tea set that his valet was no longer his acting valet.

Lips pressed tight, Donovan went over to his trunk and opened a lid. There were all his things, packed with care by Geoffrey before they had left the ducal town house. Donovan opened the doors and drawers of the armoire and transferred everything inside as neatly as he could, taking care to ensure his unmentionables did not touch Geoffrey's.

He was tempted to touch them himself. Geoffrey had seen the duke in his altogether on countless occasions, but Donovan had never glimpsed his valet in anything short of sartorial perfection. What might Geoffrey look like in nothing more than a nightshirt?

Donovan kept his fingers from straying toward the neatly folded garment. Rules were rules for a reason. They protected him.

He shut the drawer and turned to the looking-glass to run a hand through his hair. Geoffrey looked as though he'd stepped out of a fashion plate, but the duke looked like he'd spent hours trapped inside a carriage. His cravat was askew and his coat was wrinkled and his hair had sprouted five new cowlicks.

Donovan tamed his hair as best he could with a comb and a bit of water from the nightstand. Trying to right his cravat resulted in mangling the folds even more. As for his wrinkled coat, the duke did not have the least notion how to iron clothing. His appearance would have to do for now.

He paused in the doorway to the parlor. Geoffrey was seated in the center of the sofa, head back, eyes closed, his long fingers folded in his lap.

"Are you sleeping?" the duke said softly.

His valet's eyes opened. "Just thinking."

"About the festival?" Donovan asked hopefully. The festival was a safe topic. Men and women engaged in courtship. Nothing at all to do with him and Geoffrey.

"About afterwards," his valet answered.

Not after the festival, Donovan realized. After Geoffrey left the duke's employ.

"Will you return to France?" he asked as casually as he could.

Geoffrey had been a recent arrival in England when he'd first become part of the duke's household. Twenty years later, only a trace of his accent remained. The few family members he'd had were long gone, too. But that did not mean he'd continue to make this country his home. Not when a valet of his caliber could find work in a palace if he so wished.

"We'll see what happens," Geoffrey said non-committally.

Donovan's heart twisted. He had never *not* known what to do. Being a duke was easy in that sense. All peers were expected to do the same things. Take a seat in the House of Lords, take a well-connected bride, take apartments in London for the spring and spend the summer in his country estates.

There were tenants and accounts and investments and ledgers, all of which also came with pre-set expectations. Everything was prescribed. Who to dance with, who to marry, who to sit next to at the dinner table, who to bow to, which debts to pay in which order.

Donovan disliked taking risks in grand part because there was never any need to. Not when every aspect of his life had been planned for him and others like him. By the time his father died fifteen years ago, Donovan already knew exactly what to do. Everyone in his class knew everyone else and was expected to play their roles as assigned, and keep to their own kind. There was already a mold. All Donovan had to do was fill it.

He could not imagine moving to a new country. Or searching for employment. The thought of ingratiating himself with total strangers made his skin crawl. And the thought of Geoffrey bathing some other man... rubbing his feet... fastening his buttons...

White-hot jealousy galvanized Donovan's muscles. It was all he could do to grit his teeth in silence and maintain his stiff pose beside the open doorway. He needed to get out of this apartment before his wayward thoughts drove him mad.

He retrieved a folded paper from an inner pocket. It was as wrinkled as Donovan's coat, but still perfectly legible. "The innkeeper was kind enough to provide us with a map of the town, but assured me one need only follow the flood of people in the direction of noise and laughter."

A grin lit Geoffrey's face. "Excellent. Let us see how much trouble we can get into."

CHAPTER 7

*T*here was indeed a river of people flowing past the front of the inn. A few sat in carriages and several rode on horseback, but most were on foot. Singly, in pairs, in groups—it didn't seem to matter. Strangers exchanged smiles and fell into step beside each other, excited about... well, *something*, apparently.

Donovan and Geoffrey waited for an opening, then stepped into the crowd and let the current sweep them along.

"What is happening?" the duke enquired of a woman on his left as he and Geoffrey strode along with the crowd.

The woman stared at Donovan as though he had just admitted to never having heard of the King of England. "Why, it's the grand unveiling!"

"Nothing's veiled," muttered the seventeen or eighteen-year-old daughter at her side. "They're flowers. Plants need sun."

"Rhubarb is sweeter without sun," countered the girl's younger brother.

58

"Not everyone is a budding Royal Botanist," the girl snapped.

"'Budding'." The boy elbowed his sister in the ribs. "Splendid play on words, poetess."

The mother ignored them both. "Today is the jubilee celebration marking fifty years of successful matchmaking—"

"'Jubilee' *means* 'fifty years'," said the girl. "And not everyone makes a match."

"Well, you might have if—" began her brother.

"It's the botanical gardens," the mother said to Donovan more loudly, trying to be heard over her bickering children. "As grand as Versailles—"

"Four hundred hectares are *half* as many as Versailles," said her daughter.

"But still impressive," put in the boy. "A hundred times the size of Vauxhall Gardens."

"*Three* hundred times the size," his sister corrected.

"You're proving my point," her brother said smugly.

"At the center of which," their mother continued, "is England's largest hedgerow labyrinth, which hides several dozen enclaves containing follies, ponds, piazzas, Chinese temples…"

"Two hundred times as unsavory as Vauxhall Gardens' Dark Walk," the boy said with sparkling eyes.

"I'm not allowed in without Mother," his sister confirmed bitterly.

"But *no one* will bother with the labyrinth until after the May King and Queen are crowned," said their mother. "That grand unveiling is the moment we've all been waiting for."

"I've been waiting for lemon ices," said the boy.

"I prefer raspberry," said the girl.

"I see," said Donovan, with a glance at his valet. "Thank you."

"There's an orchestra every afternoon and dancing every night," the mother added. "You really cannot miss any of the festivities."

"We wouldn't dream of it," said Geoffrey with a straight face.

Donovan nodded. "He came here specifically for the crowning of the May Queen."

"It could have been my Permelia," said the mother, nudging her daughter crossly. "If she would have *accepted* a certain gentleman's offer last year at this time."

"Oh dear," said Geoffrey. "Is the May Queen already spoken for?"

"Pity," said the duke, and shook his head sorrowfully.

"Each year's May Queen is the most successful match of the year before. She picks her seven favorites on the first day of the new festival, in honor of the seven days of celebrations. The young ladies become the most sought-after all week, and start the first set of dancing every night." She gave her daughter a longing look. "There's still hope for you."

"I'd rather die," the girl said flatly.

Her mother sighed. "She'd rather write poetry."

"Which is *worse* than dying, if you've ever read any of it," said the boy.

"Oh! We're here!" The mother clapped her hands. "Forgive me, gentlemen. We're off, we're off!"

She speared her way through the surging crowd, ushering her children to the front of the pack. A huge golden gate swung open, and the people spilled through like water breaking free of a dam.

Donovan and Geoffrey had no choice but to continue forward—or be trampled beneath a thousand eager feet.

Through the gate, the gardens stretched out to either side and back, endless patterns of colorful flowers in intricate geometric shapes, with clever walking paths twisting around and between each display.

At the center stood the tallest hedgerow Donovan had ever seen. Each pathway was no wider than the wingspan of his arms. He stared in wonder at the vast green labyrinth it contained. The only way to discern more would be to investigate firsthand.

None of the other guests seemed remotely interested in the labyrinth, however. The tide of spectators flowed up to a tall wooden dais. Upon this grand stage were two flower-laden brass thrones and seven equally florid wrought-iron chairs. A young man and young woman linked arms at the edge of the platform, waving energetically at the crowd with their free hands.

"Our future May King and Queen, I take it," murmured the duke.

"Perhaps even the future King and Queen of

England," Geoffrey answered, wide-eyed with faux innocence. "I'd vote for them."

The duke sniffed. "That's not how it works, you heretic."

"You're just vexed I didn't say I'd vote for *you*."

"I wouldn't want to be king," Donovan said with feeling. "I don't even want to be duke."

"*Now* who's the heretic?" Geoffrey said wryly.

"Wait. Do you know what I really am?" the duke said slowly as he glanced around the sea of faces with wonder.

"Tell me."

"Anonymous."

It felt impossible. In the House of Lords, and at his mother's parties, and everywhere in London, hundreds of pairs of eyes were trained endlessly on Donovan. Would he speak? Would he dance? Would he finally choose a bride?

Here, he was surrounded by several *thousand* people... and not one of them made a single glance in Donovan's direction. They had no idea he was a duke. They didn't care about him at all.

Oh, certainly this good fortune would change if he were foolish enough to announce that he was a bachelor in possession of a title and on the hunt for a wife. But the merrymakers could not intuit this unhappy circumstance merely by looking at him. He was in no danger of being looked at, at all.

A woman walked on stage bearing a crown of roses in each hand. A roar of approval rose up from the crowd as they surged forward.

"Are you thinking what I'm thinking?" whispered the duke.

"Raspberry ices are indeed superior to lemon ices?" guessed his valet.

Donovan grabbed Geoffrey by the elbow and did his best to tow him against the current. "This is the perfect time to enter the labyrinth. Once all these people are inside it, the labyrinth will either become too clogged to explore, or too easy to navigate because they all know the way."

"I don't know," Geoffrey said doubtfully. "A labyrinth a hundred times bigger than Vauxhall Gardens doesn't sound easy to navigate under any circumstances."

"Reluctant to be stranded alone with me in some forgotten corner of an idyllic, secluded garden?"

This time, it was Geoffrey who grabbed Donovan's arm and dragged him forward. "Good point."

They burst free from the crowd a few yards from the break in the hedgerow. No one followed them, whether on foot or with their eyes. The ceremony on stage captured the attention of all.

"Ready?" asked Geoffrey.

Donovan pretended to lift a glass of champagne. "To a holiday to remember."

Geoffrey touched his raised knuckles to Donovan's, then stepped inside the labyrinth.

Donovan ran past him as fast as he could, as if he had any idea which way he was going. He took a left at random, then a right, then another left—then burst out laughing when he found himself at a dead end, in a hedgerow-lined dead end no larger than a water closet.

"Gorgeous," said Geoffrey, stroking the faint

stubble on his strong chin. He glanced about narrow confines like a man admiring a fine painting in a museum. "I particularly like the use of green in this space. It seems more than an artistic flair, as though the designer was trying to convey a message. A message like, 'You two bumble-brains have been in this labyrinth for two minutes, and you're already lost.'"

Donovan grinned and backed out of the opening. "Race you to the next wrong turn."

He took off running without giving Geoffrey an opportunity to reply. Five lefts and four rights later, they burst shoulder-to-shoulder into another dead-end stub of the labyrinth.

"We're still lost," Donovan admitted. "But significantly further than before."

Geoffrey smiled back at him. "There's no one else I'd rather be lost with. In fact, I think it is fair to say…"

But the valet trailed off rather than explain his thought, choosing instead to gaze down at Donovan with a shadowed face.

Gazed down! At Donovan! Who measured six feet in his bare feet. An unheard-of height. He was the giant of Parliament, towering over all the other peers like a lamp post amongst candlesticks.

Donovan had long suspected that Geoffrey's height was the reason Donovan's father had hired him as valet to his gangly son. All of the rest of the required characteristics of a valet would pale next to the simple question of being able to *reach* the future duke's cravat.

Whatever his father's reasons for selecting Geoffrey, Donovan had been grateful from the very first. As Sorcha had noted, the valet was indeed singularly pleasant to look at. But Geoffrey was more than handsome. He was kind, and caring, and funny. Easygoing more often than not, yet stern when Donovan needed it. Strong as an ox and gentler than a lamb. Up for anything, from badly played chess to well-studied musical instruments. Implacable, when it came to the quality of a good shave or the inadvisability of a particularly disastrous haircut.

As Donovan's constant companion for twenty years, they'd spent more time together than most husbands and wives. And yet... they were rarely alone together outside of Donovan's private apartments. And never as equals.

Donovan had stood in front of Geoffrey, as close as this, thousands of times before. In arm's reach of temptation. And yet it had never felt so ripe and succulent. Like a plump grape just bursting with sweet juices, waiting to be tasted. The moment was electric with possibility and promise.

He lifted his hand and reached out to smooth an invisible wrinkle from Geoffrey's immaculate lapel.

But Donovan's fingertips halted a hair's-breadth away from making contact.

It was always Geoffrey who touched him, never the other way around. It was the only way contact was allowed at all. Condoned. Overlooked. Forgotten. Meaningless, save to the boy who had yearned to touch in return. Who had grown into a man that had never lost that longing. A man who wanted nothing more than to close this gap between them.

"Why do you hesitate?" Geoffrey asked, his voice husky.

Donovan stared at his trembling hand, poised just above Geoffrey's barrel chest.

"How can I press forward?" he managed, neither removing his hand nor giving in to desire.

"How can you not?" Geoffrey asked softly.

Donovan wrenched his hand back to his side. "I am a duke."

"And I am a valet. For thirteen more days." Geoffrey shrugged his big shoulders.

"I am a duke always and forever."

"I am a *man* always and forever."

"*As am I*," Donovan burst out. "That is the problem."

"Not to me." Geoffrey's gaze was frank. "Who cares?"

"Everyone cares!"

"I don't. I've no interest in kissing everyone."

"Who said anything... about..." The breath had vanished from Donovan's lungs.

Geoffrey raised his brows. "Is that not what you were contemplating with all that anguish? Or is plucking a minuscule speck of dust from my lapel so far beneath your station as to turn you into a quivering mass of jelly?"

"Let's put the question of acts of sodomy aside for a moment."

"Yes, let's," Geoffrey agreed. "'For the moment' means we may have a chance to do it later."

"You mean discuss it later?"

"Do I?"

"Damn it, Geoffrey, I am trying to be a good man! A lord… No, scratch that. This part has nothing to do with titles. An employer, regardless of other considerations, should never force his attentions on an employee."

"Is…this your idea of 'forcing' yourself upon me?"

"It's not right."

"That's nonsense."

"It's an unethical abuse of my position."

"It's unethical if the employee believes they must submit to undesirable acts in order to maintain their post, and therefore, their livelihood. I've already lost my job, if you'll recall. You dismissed me yesterday. If I let you kiss me, will you give me my post back?"

"No." The word came out garbled.

"If I refuse your attentions instead, will you restore my post then?"

"No," Donovan repeated hoarsely.

"Then we've settled that. My livelihood is in no greater jeopardy, regardless of my choices. Which you should let *me* make. In case you haven't noticed, I'm a grown man."

"I might have noticed," the duke mumbled. "On occasion."

"Then let me be one. If you wish to kiss me, then attempt to do so. I will either allow it, or I will not."

Donovan's throat went dry. "You're saying… you might *not* welcome such an overture?"

Geoffrey's gaze was steady. "Try it and find out."

Ethics aside, legalities aside, how could Donovan bear to kiss a man who would disappear from his life in less than a fortnight?

Unless that *was* the point. If not now, then when? If not with the man he'd pined for from both near and afar for twenty long years... then with whom? Some luckless chit, who would soon find herself saddled with a husband who preferred chest hair to pert breasts?

If Donovan allowed this opportunity to vanish, there would not be another. If he was ever going to attempt to make reality from his dreams, this was the moment.

Without allowing his brain another moment to talk himself out of what was likely to be a highly unwise action, Donovan grasped Geoffrey's pristine lapels, crushing them in his fists, and he pressed his lips to Geoffrey's.

The valet's lips were warm and soft, exactly as they looked. Exactly as Donovan had imagined, time and again. They melted against his, at once pliant yet urgent and demanding. Geoffrey's arms rose around Donovan's sides, gliding up the expert cut of his worsted coat until the valet's long, hot fingers cradled Donovan's face, holding him in place. Coaxing the kiss deeper.

His valet tasted of sweet tea, courtesy of the contents of Donovan's traveling bag during the long drive. His tongue was sure and dominant, stroking the duke's own in a way that Donovan could feel from the tip of his cock all the way to the base.

If it weren't for the ridiculous tightness of his pantaloons, his cock would be knocking against his valet's thigh... or perhaps against Geoffrey's own cock.

The idea sent Donovan nearly into a frenzy. He wanted to rend every well-tailored stitch from their bodies, tossing the rags to the ground before tumbling their naked bodies atop them, rolling in silk and cambric and superfine and soft grass as their hands and kisses found every inch of each other's bodies.

He wrenched his open mouth from Geoffrey's before he could lose his mind completely, here in this public garden where anyone might stumble across them.

"There," Geoffrey said softly. "Now you know what will happen if you attempt to kiss me. Think about that before you try again."

Oh, God. Donovan licked his lips. He would think of nothing else for the rest of his life.

CHAPTER 8

$\mathcal{W}$hen at last they returned to the inn, the single bed in the middle of their shared chamber no longer felt like a torture device. Donovan reached for Geoffrey as soon as the bed was in sight.

Geoffrey hesitated before returning the kiss, then gently eased out of Donovan's embrace. "I'll change in the other room if you'd like to use this one."

Oh.

They were not going to toss their clothes upon the floor and tumble onto the mattress in a tangle of limbs and wet kisses. Geoffrey's rejection was much worse than simply continuing the status quo. They had stepped over that line. Broken that barrier. Geoffrey *knew* Donovan desired him and did not feel the same.

The duke had only himself to blame. Two decades of fantasies had made him believe that sharing a kiss meant Geoffrey would wish to share everything else. But of course stolen kisses did not imply consent to lovemaking.

"I'm sorry," he said in haste. "I didn't mean to presume..."

That's what peers did, wasn't it? Presume their every whim would be granted. Money and power could acquire just about anything. In ordinary circumstances. Donovan—or rather, his title—might be irresistible to social-climbing debutantes, but what could he offer Geoffrey? Nothing. Not even a promise of employment.

"I'm your friend, remember?" Geoffrey said wryly.

For another week. After which, he would be demoted to valet until the end of the fortnight. After which... Geoffrey would be gone.

"I remember." Donovan clenched his teeth.

"And you're here to find a bride," his valet added.

"I remember," snarled the duke with considerably more ire than he intended.

It was not Geoffrey's fault. These were Donovan's own words. Donovan's own plan. Donovan's future. Who in their right mind would get involved with a man who, by his own admission, was on the hunt for and intended to marry someone else?

"When we return to London," he began.

"I shan't be your 'friend' anymore," Geoffrey answered. "Six days of valet service, and then out into the streets I go."

It sounded horrid. Conscienceless. "What if... What if we extended—"

"No." Geoffrey removed his nightshirt from the armoire. "You've given me the sack twice in the past week. A fortnight's notice is enough. I do not wish to keep extending for a few more days here and there, never knowing when the next dismissal will come. You wish me gone. I will go. That will be the end of it."

Donovan rubbed his face with his hand. Geoffrey was right, of course. Offering him another extension before his inevitable dismissal wasn't a magnanimous favor. It was selfish. Donovan grasping for a little more time of what *he* wanted, without consideration of what Geoffrey might want.

Of course his valet wouldn't wish to tiptoe around, peppering the duke with sweet kisses whilst fully aware the duke intended to send him packing the moment a well-born bride appeared in the picture.

Donovan had never wanted a bride less in his life. But he would not pressure Geoffrey to do anything that made him uncomfortable. If that meant sticking to the current plan, then so be it.

Friends. *Openly.* And perhaps kissing-friends, in private.

That would have to be enough.

～

DONOVAN AWOKE before Geoffrey every day that week.

Not because the bed was uncomfortable, but because he enjoyed watching Geoffrey sleep. And because the first thing Geoffrey did every morning was give Donovan a kiss before rising from bed to put himself in order.

Donovan was not remotely in order. Not on the outside: Tying a cravat had resulted a task far outside the capabilities of the duke's untrained fingers. And not on the inside. The stolen kisses with Geoffrey ranged from tender to torrid, but never escalated beyond kissing, leaving Donovan in a permanent state of arousal and frustration.

To his surprise, however, the festival indeed proved a sound distraction. Donovan had long believed he despised social interaction, but it appeared what he actually disliked were public appearances without Geoffrey by his side.

As long as they were together, the knot that Donovan hadn't realized he'd been carrying around all these years unraveled. He was able to relax. To smile. To pay attention to his surroundings. To enjoy them, content to finally be in the right company.

And *everyone* thought Geoffrey was the right company. His tall, muscled form and handsome face and impeccable style earned him the admiration of every woman at the festival. Most presumed Geoffrey a lord, or at least the sort of toff who rubbed shoulders with the aristocracy. His slight French accent—which grew suspiciously more pronounced when flirting with strangers—spawned rumors that perhaps he was foreign royalty.

"I could get used to this," Geoffrey teased.

He seemed more than suitable for it. He was a natural.

Donovan, on the other hand, was more overlooked by the day. If the knack of tying a fashionable cravat was outside his capabilities, shaving his own face proved positively impossible. As for wrinkles... All three of the coats Donovan had brought now displayed a mortifying iron-shaped singe in the rear.

While his valet looked like a prince, the duke looked like a pauper. He had become so unrecognizable that even his own brother had needed a second glance when they'd passed on the stairwell. At this rate, Donovan wouldn't catch a bride without kidnapping one.

Not that he was looking. He'd had eyes for no one but Geoffrey since the moment the valet had waltzed into his life. The effect was thousandfold, now that they had an intimate secret. Every day brought more kisses.

And every day brought them closer to the holiday coming to an end.

Friday came quickly. Only one day remained. To his utter surprise, Donovan truly enjoyed the May Day festival. He and Geoffrey attended every event, together, developing over the course of the short week a secret language in which they could communicate thoughts and reactions with the slightest tic of an eyebrow or quirk of the lips.

Or perhaps they'd developed this rapport over the past twenty years. With most of their previous interactions taking place alone in Donovan's private chambers, there had been no watching crowd, and therefore no particular need for subtlety.

And yet, every thought, every action, every touch had been drenched in subtlety and secrets. Two decades of unvoiced longing, hidden behind an immobile brow or the firm set of the lips, belying the vast stores of passion bubbling with the urge to break free.

Atop the pedestrian bridge curving over the duck-filled pond in the center of the labyrinth, Donovan smiled over at Geoffrey. Other merry-makers clogged the bridge and milled around the pond, sailing paper boats and tossing breadcrumbs at ducklings.

Geoffrey consulted his pocket watch. "That was our best time yet."

"I knew we could do it."

He and Geoffrey had forged this path every day for a week, and could now make their way to many of the artfully hidden follies without a single wrong turn.

Not that this hard-earned knowledge stopped them from taking wrong turns on *purpose*, dipping into dead-ends at strategic moments to steal a quick kiss.

"Are you thinking what I'm thinking?" Donovan asked.

Geoffrey's eyes heated. "Make the return take twice as long?"

"Thrice."

They threaded through the crowd and loped across the garden to the hedgerows, their shoulders brushing as they ducked back into the shadowy coolness of the tall labyrinth.

Now that the truth was out in the open between them... Now that the pining was no longer clandestine, but rather reciprocated and acted upon... *All* ordinary tasks required double or triple the time.

A kiss accompanied every new fold of the cravat, every button penetrating its hole, every swipe of the razor—leaving Geoffrey with bits of white froth from shaving soaps clinging to his lips and chin.

As to the festival, well. Despite attending every event without fail, Donovan still hadn't the least notion who had been chosen as this year's attendants. It was the company that made the holiday so fine, not their surroundings. He suspected he could attend a symposium on horse manure with Geoffrey at his side and enjoy every minute of it.

But Marrywell was not real life. A small part of Donovan was constantly aware that his holiday here was just that: a welcome but short-lived respite from the world and the realities and the duties he must soon return to. A flash of lightning, bright and fleeting.

"Will we be attending tonight's farewell ball?" Geoffrey asked when at last they emerged from the hedgerow labyrinth.

Donovan assented. Not just because his brother and sister-in-law would be in attendance and expect to see the duke among the crush, but also because Donovan had promised himself not to miss sharing a single activity with Geoffrey.

"Will you be dancing?" Geoffrey asked.

Donovan made a face. If he could not waltz with Geoffrey, then he would not dance with anyone.

"There will be a surplus of beautiful women to choose from," Geoffrey reminded him with a remarkably serious expression.

"If you say so," Donovan muttered.

Although Geoffrey frequently remarked upon the presence of this beauty or that, Donovan had eyes for no one but Geoffrey. No other form, man or woman, could hold a candle.

An insidious thought occurred to him. "Will *you* be dancing tonight?"

CHAPTER 9

*G*eoffrey stared at him as though he, too, had forgotten until this moment that he was attending the festivities as an independently moneyed gentleman, rather than as manservant to a lord. If he wanted to dance, he could. With any woman he pleased. Donovan—or his brother—would make the introductions as if the duke's stomach wasn't churning with unreasonable jealousy at the sight of Geoffrey taking someone else into his arms, if only for a public, twenty-minute set.

"If you are not dancing, neither shall I," was all Geoffrey said.

It did not answer the question of whether he *wished* to. Of whether the comments about pretty young ladies were meant for Donovan's benefit, or expressing the direction of Geoffrey's own desires. Donovan only found men attractive, but that did not mean Geoffrey suffered the same limitation. Nor were there any promises between them. No ground to stand on to prevent Geoffrey from engaging in some other flirtation, be it with gentleman or lady.

After all, they were here to select Donovan a bride.

No. He could not ruin this holiday. The bride could wait until after Geoffrey left his employ, so as to fully enjoy every remaining moment of his company.

"An early supper?" Donovan asked.

Geoffrey pantomimed fainting relief. "Posthaste. Which tavern shall we try this evening?"

"We've not yet frequented the Cork & Cupid."

"Let us rectify that error at once."

They turned their boots toward the main street through town.

Instead of smiling in anticipation, Donovan clenched his teeth in trepidation. This was the final night of the festival, and one of the last nights he would ever share with Geoffrey.

Yes, Donovan *could* offer his valet his post back. He might be able to persuade Geoffrey to accept a permanent position. But that would only reinstate the return of years of misery in which Geoffrey would be close enough to touch, yet forever out of reach.

Once there was a wife on the premises, Donovan was not so shabby a man as to contemplate cuckolding her. He would be the best husband he could, just as he made every effort to be the best duke as he was able.

No matter how he calculated, the result was

always the same: He and Geoffrey could not be together.

"How many are ye?" asked a harried serving girl when they entered the tavern.

"Two, please," responded Donovan.

"You're doubly in luck." She pointed with a dish rag. "There's naught but two seats left, and they're right next to the musicians, who'll be starting their show at any moment."

"'Show'?" Donovan repeated with curiosity.

"Got to compete with the grand ball, don't we? No room for an orchestra, but we can fit a pair of violinists."

"Violins!" Geoffrey exclaimed, smiling at Donovan with warm eyes.

Musical evenings had long been a private entertainment of theirs. Not only was this deprivation yet one more pleasure soon to be denied them, but also a circumstance even worse for Geoffrey, who did not own a violin of his own. Donovan reminded himself not to let Geoffrey leave without carrying away the better of the two instruments.

They eased their large frames into the sole remaining seats and placed their supper orders moments before the musicians lifted their violins to their chins and launched into melody and harmony.

The traveling duo were perhaps not virtuosos, and their musical choices tended more to the vulgar than to Bach and Mozart, but the rousing music was uplifting and energetic, and in no time at all, the tavern patrons were stomping their feet along with the rhythm.

Scarcely an hour had passed when one of the customers called out, "We want a sailor's song!"

Cries of assent echoed throughout the noisy tavern. The rhyming lyrics to sailors' songs were notorious for being overly emotional and un-apologetically bawdy.

Donovan and Geoffrey exchanged glances.

"Are you thinking what I'm thinking?" Geoffrey asked, his eyes sparkling.

"I hope not," Donovan said grimly.

"Oh, come on, you spoilsport." Geoffrey leapt atop his wooden stool. "We'll play the accompaniment, if our esteemed musicians will sing the words!"

The closest violinist cradled his instrument to his chest as though protecting a newborn baby.

"Can you play?" asked his skeptical companion.

"A bit. Not as well as *him*." The tip of Geoffrey's boot nudged Donovan in the ribs. "He's known as... the Sultan of Strings!"

Donovan snorted into his mug of ale. "The *what*?"

"Get him on his feet, then," said the violinist, handing over his instrument. "The lads have asked for a tune. Do you know..." He named the lewdest song ever to be sung in a tavern.

"The Sultan practically invented it," Geoffrey assured him, barely hiding his laughter as he curved his fingers beneath Donovan's arms and hauled him to his feet. "Come on then. Don't be shy, Sultan."

"I will kill you," Donovan informed him.

"Kill me after the song." Geoffrey handed him a violin, then placed the other beneath his own chin. Without giving Donovan further opportunity to complain or demur, Geoffrey scraped his bow across two of the strings, then launched into the accompanist's melody.

With a sigh, Donovan placed his feet more squarely on the wooden stool, then lowered his bow to the strings. Normally, he would have fussed with tuning the instrument and applying rosin to the bow first, but there was no time, nor was this the crowd for scruples.

He allowed the primary melody to burst forth from the violin instead, wrenching from it notes high and pure, then low and lusty, racing back and forth with ever-increasing speed and volume until the entire tavern was on its feet cheering in approval.

They played for over an hour, everyone growing more tipsy and the lyrics becoming less intelligible with every new song. The barmaids kept the ales coming for Dominic and Geoffrey, not that there was time to do more than grab a hurried sip between pieces before beginning anew.

Yet somehow, by the time they returned the violins to their rightful owners and begged their leave from a roaring and adoring crowd, Donovan was anything but sober. He and Geoffrey stumbled back to the inn with their arms about each other's shoulders, hip to drunken hip, half-remembered words still warbling from their mouths.

Perhaps that was why Donovan pulled Geoffrey into their shared chamber—and his embrace. Perhaps that was why Geoffrey responded by kicking the door closed and crushing his lips to Donovan's.

Or perhaps it had always been inevitable, and they had only wanted an excuse to allow them to realize their desires.

They did not to take the kisses into the bedroom, not that the tiny parlor with its convenient chaise provided much deterrent to carnal acts. But rather than tumble onto its soft surface, Geoffrey backed Donovan against the wall instead, pinning his shoulders to the wallpaper and trapping his hands up above either side of his head.

Soon, Donovan broke free, finally allowing his hands to roam hungrily over Geoffrey's arms and shoulders and chest.

Geoffrey responded by tossing Donovan's cravat aside, then freeing button after button.

Donovan skipped over Geoffrey's coat and waistcoat and headed straight to the fall of his trousers instead. Those were the buttons that most interested him. The treasure he wished most to unveil. His fingers were clumsy compared to the valet's, but he managed to free half of the fall.

Geoffrey's skilled fingers followed suit, his outsized hand closing around Donovan's painfully rigid shaft at the same moment that Donovan's fingers encircled Geoffrey's own.

They stroked as they kissed, gasping into each

other's mouths as they stoked the fire burning between them into an inferno of desire. Donovan could no longer keep his cock from bucking with pleasure inside Geoffrey's silken grip. Wet heat covered Donovan's own fingers as Geoffrey's seed spilled from his shaft.

Afterwards, they touched their sweaty foreheads together, panting. Realization of the line they had just crossed slowly crept into their consciousness.

"I took advantage," Donovan croaked.

"I took what I wanted," Geoffrey countered.

"We should not have—" the duke began again.

"—stopped there," his valet finished.

A strangled laugh escaped Donovan's throat. "An excellent point. Very well. Next time?"

Geoffrey grinned. "Next time."

Donovan was done denying himself. He intended to enjoy every moment.

CHAPTER 10

$\mathcal{C}$ome morning, the duke's coach-and-four was ready and waiting in front of the inn... along a street with hundreds of other carriages likewise awaiting their owners for a long journey home.

"It's going to take six hours just to inch out of Marrywell," observed Donovan, standing in front of the inn.

"It was worth it," gushed his sister-in-law, gazing up at her husband, whose arm she clutched adoringly.

Bernard responded with an indulgent kiss to the tip of Sorcha's upturned nose.

She smiled at him, then turned her startled gaze toward Donovan. "At least, I hope it was worth it for all of us. Did you gentlemen find what you came for?"

"I certainly found... a big part," Geoffrey responded with a straight face. "A very big part."

Good breeding prevented Donovan from favoring his valet with a sharp elbow to the ribs.

"What about you, brother?" asked Bernard. "Did you find the woman of your dreams?"

"Not yet," Donovan replied carefully.

"Oh, Southbury." His sister-in-law placed a consoling palm on his arm. "I'm so sorry."

"Please do not be. I am perfectly happy."

"You know... I think you might be," Bernard said in surprise, tilting his head as he peered at his brother. "I've seen you smile more today than I have in the past decade, and I haven't seen you all week."

"Perhaps that's why he's finally happy," Sorcha whispered. "Without his overbearing little brother around to henpeck him."

"Me?' Bernard sputtered. "*You* are the one who insisted we should not rest until Southbury was settled as happily as you and I. Why, the night before Mother's supper party, it was you who turned to me and said—"

"Look, our carriage is ready." Cheeks flushing pink, Sorcha dragged her husband toward the waiting coachman and waved her fingers over her shoulder at Donovan and Geoffrey. "Thank you for a lovely week!"

Donovan watched them go in wonder. He had assumed his family would be upset—or at least deeply concerned—if he did not marry, but if Bernard didn't give a fig, and all Donovan's family wanted was for Donovan to be happy...

He turned to Geoffrey. "What do you think it was that Sorcha said to Bernard?"

"'I'd wager ten quid the duke's valet has a raging cockstand when he bathes his master.'"

Donovan pushed Geoffrey up into the coach. "She hadn't met you at that point."

"It doesn't matter. She should have extrapolated from context. One look at your muscular form, and *any* man with a cock could reasonably find it difficult to keep his pants buttoned. At least, that's been my experience whenever I'm in the same room as you. Oh, look, we're sharing the same space right now!" He fluttered his eyelashes in faux surprise. "There grows my cock."

Donovan's throat dried. Could that be true? Had Donovan been desperately tamping down his own erections for years, never realizing the valet beside him suffered from the same condition? In that case, it wasn't the alcohol that had set the night's activities in motion. It was Donovan himself. Geoffrey had been interested all along.

Head spinning, Donovan banged on the connecting panel to signal the driver before settling back on the squab.

Geoffrey took the seat opposite him.

These were the same positions they'd assumed on the journey west, but the atmosphere inside the carriage felt different this time. Cozier, perhaps, as though they were a comfortable married couple relaxing before a fire, instead of the usual master-and-servant on tenterhooks, viscerally aware of each other, yet forbidden from acknowledging the electricity crackling between them.

"I hope you brought lukewarm tea in a whiskey flask," said Geoffrey. "And a heavy stack of accounting journals. Lord, do I love relaxing with four hundred pages of spindly columns of endless numbers. Especially if I have a carrot stick to munch on, as if I were a horse. Nothing is more satisfying than—"

"I did bring a gag this time," Donovan warned him. "Don't tempt me."

"I bet you didn't," said Geoffrey.

"It's my cravat," Donovan countered. "I will shove it into your mouth at the least provocation."

"And ruin my craftsmanship?" Geoffrey gasped. "You monster!"

"Like I said." Donovan lifted his chin. "Don't tempt me."

"Or what?" Geoffrey asked innocently. "You'll shove something else into my mouth?"

The idea was more than tempting.

"*Now* which one of us has the raging cock-stand," Donovan muttered.

"We do have six hours before we're back in London," Geoffrey pointed out. "Six long... hard... turgid hours."

Donovan shook his finger at him. "The privacy of a bedchamber is one thing. But I will not be caught with my pants down in a moving carriage."

"The odds of a traffic accident—"

"—are the highest they've ever been," the duke finished dryly. "We are in a tight queue with a thousand other carriages. Men on horseback regularly glance through the window as they pass. I'm fairly certain I just saw someone's grandmother *walk* past the glass."

"There are curtains for a reason," Geoffrey grumbled. "If they are insufficient, we should have left in the dark of night."

"And miss the grand ball?" the duke asked wryly.

"We did miss the grand ball."

"Because we were entertaining each other in my apartment's closet-sized sitting room instead," said Donovan. "Are you sorry to have missed the highlight of the holiday?"

"I *didn't* miss the highlight of my holiday," his valet replied softly.

"In that case, I believe all that dancing requires a restorative foot massage," the duke announced.

Geoffrey closed the curtain and started to ease off of his seat to attend to the task.

Donovan beat him to the floor, sliding to his knees before his valet's spread legs.

"What are you doing?" Geoffrey asked in alarm.

"I just told you."

Carefully, Donovan eased the flawlessly shined boots from his valet's enormous feet, then lifted one of the warm, silk-stockinged feet onto his thighs.

"I've never given a foot massage before," he said gruffly. "Forgive me if I am imperfect."

"I'm already hard," Geoffrey whispered back. "You're doing a great job."

Donovan worked his thumbs gently into the pad of Geoffrey's foot, doing his best to emulate the strokes and pressure that had brought him the most pleasure at the hands of his valet.

Geoffrey groaned as his eyes fluttered closed and his head lolled back against the padded panel.

ERICA RIDLEY

Donovan's hands glided over the silk, stroking, kneading, soothing. "How am I doing?"

"Never stop."

The duke grinned. "We could have been taking turns all along if I'd had any inkling you were interested in me."

"Any inkling! I bathed you *naked* and you gave no sign that my ministrations affected you in the least."

"You have no idea the mental effort required to keep my cock from springing up in your presence, whether you're touching me or not."

"If you had let it fly, I might have rubbed more than your feet."

"I wish I would have," Donovan said wryly.

His stomach flipped to think how different the past two decades might have been if he hadn't tried so hard to hide his attraction to Geoffrey. Donovan kicked himself at the idea that he had no one to blame but himself for the years of agony and misery and torment.

At least the question of mutual desire had finally been put to rest.

Nearly a quarter hour had passed when he eased Geoffrey's foot aside and picked up the other in order to massage it with the same gentle care.

"Marry me," Geoffrey murmured.

Donovan chuckled. "Not allowed, I'm afraid."

"I'll wear a petticoat and a bonnet."

"Something about your hulking, six-foot-five frame makes me think it would take more than a skirt and bonnet to disguise all that manliness."

Donovan's voice softened. "And I wouldn't want to. I like looking at you just as you are."

Geoffrey's eyes flickered open, hooded and aroused. "I like everything about you. Even your terrible choices in carriage refreshments."

"You'd do this again?"

"I'd go anywhere with you. You must know this by now."

Donovan lowered his gaze to Geoffrey's foot rather than respond.

Yes, he supposed he did know that by now. Had known it for some time. Knew his own feelings on the matter were much the same. Perhaps even more fervent.

All the more reason why dismissing Geoffrey from his post was the only responsible decision.

Donovan could not be *trusted* to keep his hands off his valet in the future. Not after tasting the forbidden fruit, and learning precisely what he was denying himself. His only hope of being a halfway decent husband was by removing all other temptation.

No matter if it felt like drowning in an endless pool of despair.

CHAPTER 11

To Donovan's frustration, he had no sooner returned to London than he was called away to deal with various ducal duties. The country tenants had a problem that needed to be dealt with, and tracking progress on the issues he voted on in Parliament required every moment of his waking hours for several days. There was barely a moment to sneak a kiss with his valet, much less engage in meaningful conversation.

A knock sounded on the study door.

It was not Geoffrey. Geoffrey entered rooms silently, and besides, he and all the other servants on this floor knew the duke was not to be interrupted. Which meant this was one of the downstairs footmen, bringing up yet another delivery of the post.

Donovan did not look up from the urgent letter he was writing. "If those are magazines, set them on the sideboard with the others. If it's correspondence, place it atop the pile at the corner of my desk."

"It's neither, I'm afraid," said a wry female voice.

Donovan felt his hackles rise even before he glanced up from his writing. "Mother. I do not have the time—"

"You don't have time for your mother, but you do have time for..." She moved toward the sideboard. "...fashion magazines?"

"They're for Geoffrey," Donovan muttered.

"Ah, yes. The French valet." Without being invited, Mother took a seat in front of Donovan's desk. "If those outside of this household had any idea how much time you spend with a servant, they might find your comportment unseemly."

Donovan set down his plume and crossed his arms. "They just might."

"I know I'm interrupting," his mother said quickly.

"And yet, here you are. Some might find such comportment unseemly. I've a speech to give in the House of Lords in less than three hours, and I—"

"Darling, I *know* you're busy. You're always busy. It's just... Even a busy man can find the time to take a wife. It's been two decades. I hoped when you went to Marrywell with your brother that you might find happiness—"

"I *did* find happiness."

"But not a bride!" She threw up her hands as if at her wits' end.

Donovan felt much the same. His frustration could not fully be blamed on his mother's current interruption and constant machinations, however.

She was only doing what society said good mothers ought to do. It was Donovan who was failing to uphold his role in the play.

He could not do anything about having inherited a dukedom. But he *could* decide what sort of duke he intended to be. The one society expected? Or a man who, as his mother phrased it, sought happiness?

"I am no longer on the hunt for a bride," he said softly.

Joy lit her face. "You *found* one?"

"I did not."

Confusion lined her brow.

"I've no intent to take a bride, now or ever," Donovan said gently. "If you truly wish for me to find happiness, then please understand that I am much happier now than I would be in some loveless marriage."

"I never wished you a loveless future!"

"And, with luck, I shan't have one. As much as it pains me to once again disappoint you, I fear I shall not be providing you with another daughter-in-law. Bernard has done his duty with grandchildren. At least one of us have lived up to your expectations. It shall have to be enough."

"Oh, darling. Look at you, with your piles of correspondence and shelves of duty and sleepless smudges of purple beneath your eyes. How can you believe yourself a disappointment when you constantly outperform every other peer in all ways but one?"

"The most important one," he reminded her dryly.

"No." Mother reached across the desk to take his hands, smudging the fresh ink of his letter in the process.

Donovan gritted his teeth and tried not to grimace. The letter would have to be rewritten, and now there was only a short window in which he could—wait. What had his mother just said?

"Securing the line *isn't* the most sacred duty of all?" he asked carefully.

"As you pointed out, Bernard has managed that part already. Did I hope for more grandchildren? Of course. But even more important is ensuring the happiness of *my* children. If you would rather postpone marriage for a few more years—"

"Or never bother at all?"

"Or...never bother at all," she repeated with a sigh, "I won't say another word, if you swear to me this choice brings you peace."

"It does," Donovan said firmly. "Peace and joy."

"Practically Christmas," his mother said with an odd little smile. "What else could a mother ask for besides joy for her children?" She let go of Donovan's hands and rose to her feet.

"That's it?" he asked in surprise. "No further argument?"

"I suspect the battle was lost long ago." She paused at the doorway to glance over her shoulder at him. "I should have listened the first three hundred times you said you didn't want a bride. I was so certain all you needed was to find the right person. But Bernard said..."

Donovan's throat tightened. "What did my brother say?"

"He said you already did." She stepped out into the corridor. "Give my regards to Geoffrey."

The door closed behind her before Donovan could formulate a response.

She knew. Or at least, she suspected. And this was her way of telling him that she would not stop him from pursuing love, however that might look. That his family valued Donovan's happiness over society's expectations. That he had, indeed, found the right person.

Which meant the only question that remained was how to make Geoffrey stay. Donovan wanted to woo him, to spend every remaining hour begging on his knees, but his duties conspired against him. There was no time to sleep, much less for romance.

It was Geoffrey's final night under Donovan's roof when at last he could put down his pen, step away from his desk, and have a moment to breathe without the weight of his endless responsibilities smothering him like a thick blanket.

A glance out of the study window indicated night had fallen. Donovan had once again taken his supper at his desk—a terrible habit that consisted mostly of half-remembered sandwiches and spoonfuls of tepid soup—in order to have done with his duties as quickly as possible.

He strode quickly from his study to his private quarters, eager to put work behind him and spend what remained of the evening with Geoffrey, who would be leaving on the morrow. And this time, Donovan would not be chasing behind his valet to beg for one more fortnight.

He had already asked, and Geoffrey had politely, but firmly, declined. He did not wish to skulk about in constant trepidation of receiving the sack for a third time. And who could blame him? Geoffrey deserved so much more.

Tonight, what Donovan could offer him was pleasure.

He turned the door handle, stepped into his bedchamber, and smiled at Geoffrey. Donovan's footmen had preceded him, as requested.

This evening, there was not one, but *two* side-by-side bathing tubs in the dressing room.

If his staff found this request odd—as they must—it was at least no stranger than the countless tales Donovan had heard from his peers about the luxuries and inanities they demanded of their own servants.

That the Duke of Southbury should decide to bathe twice in succession was certainly less alarming than the bathing rituals allegedly practiced by the vain Countess of Bathory, and far less taxing than the round-the-clock army of servants required to keep up with the relentless decadence and bacchanalia of the Prince Regent.

Regardless of how his peccadilloes ranked in comparison, Donovan had always paid his employees well for their continued discretion. He rarely comported himself in any manner that might raise an eyebrow, but nonetheless had always felt *prevention* of potential scandal a far wiser path than having to publicly defend his actions after the fact.

He was therefore known not just as a remarkably fair employer, but also an extraordinarily generous one. His housekeeper received dozens of new applicants every day, and turned them all away, because no servant in the duke's employ wished to leave their post before retirement.

For that reason, the day he hired a replacement for Geoffrey would be An Event within the household. The first new employee in years. Geoffrey would be the only manservant to leave before his hair had gone gray.

The irony was, Donovan no longer wanted him to go. It was Geoffrey who now agreed that the current situation could not continue. He did not trust that Donovan would not change his mind in the future, and decide anew that it was time to take a bride and rid himself of his valet.

Which meant change was inevitable.

Donovan was not looking forward to the hiring process. No matter the new hire's competence and years of experience, the man could not compare in the least. This was by design. Donovan intended to select the most dour-faced, English, physically unattractive, unimaginably dull, extremely-uninterested-in-the-charms-of-men, only-here-for-the-extravagant-salary candidate he could find.

But that was a task for tomorrow. A full night of Geoffrey's company still remained.

Donovan thanked his footmen and waited for them to leave, before he locked the bedchamber door and turned to face his valet.

His. For a few hours longer.

Geoffrey gestured toward the twin tubs. "Feeling dirty, your grace?"

"Hoping you do, too."

The flash of heat in his valet's eyes was the only answer Donovan needed.

As always, Geoffrey was dressed in the latest fashions, impeccable from tousled brown head to Hessian-clad toe, his solid form concealed from view by layers of linen and silk and wool.

Donovan would soon change that.

They met each other halfway, big hands fumbling at small buttons in their excitement, fastidious cravats and fussy little handkerchiefs flying across the dressing room with absolutely no attention paid to how or where the expensive scraps of silk and linen landed.

The coats came off, adieu, who needs you? Not with a gorgeous fire roaring in the grate, two massive bathtubs filled with steaming water, and the heat they'd kept hidden inside bursting to be set free.

Waistcoats were the next to litter the floor, then white cambric shirts. Then black boots and silk stockings, until the men stood before each other wearing only easy-to-doff trousers with nothing at all underneath.

"May I?" asked Geoffrey.

"Only if I may, as well," answered the duke.

Ridiculous to feel suddenly shy. Geoffrey had seen him naked innumerous times over the past two decades, and his valet's cock had been in Donovan's hand just five days prior.

Yet that had been unplanned. Two men in their cups, laughing like children after their escapade performing bawdy songs at a seedy tavern, falling into each other's arms with the grace of elephants and the self-control of a hurricane.

This was a seduction.

Donovan added perfumed salts to the baths, sent pink petals floating atop the water. He lit an inordinate number of candles, so as not to miss a single moment.

Geoffrey closed the gap between them and reached for Donovan's fall. The duke waited his turn, then did the same. Hand in hand, they gingerly stepped into the pools of hot, fragrant water and sank until their hips disappeared below the surface.

"Me first," the duke said hoarsely. "I can't wait any longer."

His valet reached for a wash cloth.

Donovan took it from his hand. "No. Me first."

He tossed the cloth into the basin and let it sink beneath the rose petals. Donovan wanted nothing but soap and water between his hands and Geoffrey's body.

Donovan gloried in each touch, reveling in the ability to finally explore every inch of his valet's large, muscular form.

Geoffrey did not hold still for long. His hands found a second bar of soap, as his lips sought Donovan's. Water sloshed all about them as they caressed each other with slippery fingers over naked flesh.

It didn't take long for their hands to abandon

the task of cleanliness and to find employment in exploring each other's bodies and stroking each other's shafts instead. Knowing what was coming did nothing to dampen their ardor. Their flesh burned hotter, their kisses ever more demanding, until they were in danger of repeating their release like the time before.

"Not yet," the duke gasped, and leapt from the tub. "Come with me."

"Shall we dry off first?"

"I can't wait that long." He tugged Geoffrey up from the water and out of the dressing room to the bedchamber. "Get into bed."

"At once, your grace."

But Geoffrey did not allow himself to be tumbled onto the mattress. Instead, he placed Donovan's hands overhead on one of the bedposts, the duke's naked chest facing outwards. Geoffrey then dragged a line of kisses from the corner of Donovan's mouth, along his jaw, down the straining tendons of his neck, over the muscles of his chest. He paused only to flick his tongue against Donovan's nipples before continuing on down the hard planes of the duke's abdomen, the dip above his thighs, then at last took Donovan's member into his mouth.

Donovan was certain he was going to expire from pleasure. It took every ounce of his will to keep his white-knuckled grip fast on the bedposts, rather than dig his fingers into Geoffrey's hair and pin him to Donovan's groin. The muscles of his buttocks tightened from the effort to keep from spending all at once, but before long his hips were bucking of their own accord, no longer able to keep still as he made love to the warm wet heat of Geoffrey's mouth.

Geoffrey responded by going faster, deeper. He gripped the duke's buttocks, harshly at first, then slid the tip of his finger between them.

"If you do that... I'll... I'm already..."

The moment he was penetrated, Donovan exploded in pleasure. Geoffrey did not cease his attentions until the last shockwaves subsided, then wasted no time in turning the duke around and pushing his chest forward onto the mattress, leaving the duke's arse in the air and his strong legs spread wide.

Barely a second passed before Donovan felt something warm and slick drizzling over his flesh. A disbelieving smile tugged at his lips.

"You stashed a bottle of oil beneath my mattress?"

"I've kept tiny bottles of oil stashed in every corner of your apartment for twenty years, just in case."

Geoffrey's large hands worked the oil into Donovan's skin, then drizzled extra between his buttocks. His hard, oiled shaft pressed against the duke's flesh as Geoffrey bent over Donovan's spine to press hot kisses along the back of his neck.

"May I?" he rasped.

"What are you waiting for?" Donovan growled back. Already his insatiable cock was showing signs of hardening again.

Geoffrey slid his oil-slicked hand beneath

Donovan's stomach and found the evidence for himself. With one hand coaxing Donovan's shaft back to life and the other hand gripping Donovan's hip, Geoffrey slowly eased himself into place.

In no time, they found their rhythm. They were both grunting and panting, flesh slapping against flesh, when Geoffrey cried out.

"I can't hold back any more," he gasped. "You're too... This is so..."

"Do it," Donovan ordered him. "I'm close."

Geoffrey shuddered and spent himself at once, driving fast and deep. When he finished, he pulled free and turned Donovan around, taking the duke into his mouth to capture Donovan's climax once again.

As soon as Donovan could breathe, he hauled Geoffrey up and into the bed beside him, their large bodies taking up most of the frame even as they entwined their limbs and took each other into their arms.

"That was very unethical of you," Geoffrey murmured into Donovan's neck.

The duke choked out a laugh. "Shut up."

"You know how to make me."

Donovan kissed him, threading his fingers through the softness of Geoffrey's hair, trailing the pad of his thumb across the hint of stubble at his jaw. Sleeping with him tonight was going to be just as magical as making love with him had been.

"I'd been dreading the morning," the duke said, "but you've just given me a reason to look forward to it."

A mischievous smile curved on Geoffrey's face. "Just one reason? Humph. I suppose I shall have to work... harder."

Donovan chuckled and gave him a soft kiss. "You can count on it."

CHAPTER 12

The next morning, Donovan made love to Geoffrey, then ordered breakfast to his bedchamber. Not simply to prolong the time he had with Geoffrey. But because Donovan had decided not to let him go.

Not without a fight.

Donovan had been awake all night, alternately watching Geoffrey sleep and doing his best to arrange an offer the duke hoped his valet would be unable to refuse.

Pensively, Geoffrey set down his tea cup and brushed invisible lint from his trousers. "I suppose it's time for me to go."

"Not yet." Donovan poured them both more tea.

Geoffrey furrowed his dark brows. "Are you trying to extend my employment by another fortnight?"

"I am not," Donovan assured him.

"Then I fear *I* shall not extend the pain of separation by forcing us both to endure a protracted

ERICA RIDLEY

goodbye. Unless there is some reason for me to tarry?"

"I'd like to think there might be. May I have one last moment of your time before you go?"

Geoffrey's brow furrowed in confusion, but he held up a palm in acquiescence. "By all means, your grace. I am, as ever, at your command."

"I'd like to change that."

Donovan moved his cup and saucer aside and withdrew a rolled document from beneath his coat.

"That wasn't there when I dressed you," Geoffrey said.

"It arrived with the toast and eggs."

"What is it?"

"Something I put into motion at dawn." Donovan held the scroll out for Geoffrey.

His valet did not take it.

"What is it?" he repeated, his voice tight with apprehension.

"I hope, an answer to our predicament. Did you enjoy playing the role of independent gentleman with me during our holiday?"

"You know I did."

"What if you didn't have to pretend?" Donovan shook the scroll. "Take it."

Geoffrey accepted the parchment with obvious unease. "What have you done?"

"Even a duke, with all the position's advantages, cannot make our stations equal. But I *can* give you your independence."

"You mean my dismissal."

"I don't want you to be my valet, Geoffrey. I want you to be *mine*."

"That's all you had to say."

"I don't want to command you. Not like that. I want us to be each other's to command. I want to go to bed every night in your arms, and wake up every morning with you in mine."

"What about your future duchess?"

"My bride does not exist. Has never existed for me. She is a fictional personage in certain family members' imaginations. You may have the adjoining rooms yourself, if you like."

"Certain family members who do not imagine a valet as private consort to the Duke of Southbury. Your mother, specifically."

"My mother loves me and wants me to be happy."

It felt odd to say the words aloud. Revolutionary, to realize that they were true. That it meant Donovan need not adhere to Society's rules and expectations.

But they still needed to be addressed.

"As to my valet, you've been dismissed, remember? You are no longer an employee. I am happy to tell others you are an invited guest in my home, but I would be happier still if you were to think of it as your home, as well."

Geoffrey frowned. "And when you never father an heir?"

"You're right. That *would* be a concern… if Bernard hadn't seen to the task for me. His sons are hale and healthy and will someday have sons of their own. The dukedom is secure for generations. The line does not require a lifetime of my misery with an equally miserable wife in order to survive. Indeed, we will all get on much better if I avoid that fate."

"But how will you explain yourself?"

"To strangers, I won't have to. I'm the Duke of Southbury. I answer to no one, save the royal family, and Prinny is far more concerned about the renovations on his holiday home in Brighton than he is about the details of my bedsport."

"And to those who are not strangers?"

"I shall inform my loved ones that I do not, in fact, intend to seek a bride, and that from now on, I shall be instructing Bernard and his lads in all the things they will need to know for the day when one of them inevitably must take the helm."

Geoffrey didn't look convinced. "What if they argue?"

"'Oh dear heavens, please don't consign me to the highest peerage in the land and all the pots of money that come with it'? An unlikely reaction. *I* am the one who chafed against the responsibilities of this role, and only because it prevented me from seeking happiness with you."

"Which is something this paper is going to fix?" Geoffrey lifted the scroll.

"Open it and see." Donovan held his breath. He hoped this worked.

Geoffrey hesitated, then unrolled the parchment. He scanned its contents quickly, then did so again a second time, taking each word in slowly as though that would help to make its meaning sink in.

His long fingers shook. "This… is a bank draft."

The duke inclined his head. "A severance payment, if you will. To a new account, in your name. I don't care what others want. What matters to me is what *you* want. Your happiness is my priority."

His erstwhile valet gazed down at the document with obvious incredulity. "This is my severance payment. You deposited a vail with three trailing zeroes?"

Donovan nodded. "I love you, Geoffrey. Regardless of what happens between us, I wanted you to be able to live a comfortable life, without ever having to work again. If you enjoy being a valet, by all means, continue to act as one. But if you'd prefer to be a gentleman of leisure… That is now your prerogative as well."

Geoffrey lowered his hand and stared at the duke in consternation. "This isn't enough money for me to live an ordinary life."

Donovan's gut clenched. One simple romantic gesture, and he'd bungled it!

"It's not?" he stammered.

"Of course it's not." Geoffrey lifted the bank draft and shook it. "This is enough blunt for me to spend a full season playing the role of nouveau riche bachelor elbowing his way into polite society to scoop up this season's diamond."

The duke's stomach churned for a new reason. "Is that what you want?"

"You beautiful, proud fool. I love you, too." Geoffrey tossed the parchment aside and jerked Donovan toward him by his lapels. "I have everything I want right here in my hands."

Their mouths crashed together, and their arms wound around each other tight.

"Is that a yes?" Donovan murmured against Geoffrey's mouth when they came up for air.

"I'm still deciding," Geoffrey answered. "Try harder to convince me."

"Did you say... 'harder'?" Grinning wickedly, Donovan placed the breakfast trays on the floor next to the bed. "I may indeed have a stronger argument that might convince you."

Geoffrey's eyes lit with anticipation. "Tell me more."

"I'll show you." The duke's smile widened. "By the way, I found the rest of your secret oil supply."

"And what will you do with all those riches?"

"What *we* will do," the duke corrected him gently, "is whatever the devil we *wish* to do, now and for the rest of our lives."

And so they did.

≈

≈

Keep turning for more goodies!

UNTITLED

Want more LGBTQ Regency romcoms?

~

What if Cinderella fell for the handsome prince's... sister?

Her Princess at Midnight

~

A proper Society miss recruits a very improper lady investigator in a quest for vengeance... and finds love instead!

The Perks of Loving a Wallflower

~

Enjoy sneak peeks of both books in the next pages!

HER PRINCESS AT MIDNIGHT

Cynthia lives a life of drudgery, toiling for her stepmother and stepsisters without receiving gratitude or pay. Every day is the same... until a royal retinue sweeps into town, inviting every unwed maiden to vie for the hand of the visiting prince. The moment she lays eyes on the prince's beautiful sister, Cynthia is smitten. She's never been to a ball, and she's determined not to miss this one. But when her family refuses to allow her to attend —not that Cynthia even has a gown to wear—it will take a miracle to escape the attic and catch the eye of the princess who holds the key to her heart!

CHAPTER 1

*M*iss Cynthia Talbott's muscles ached from spending the hours since dawn down on her hands and knees, scrubbing the floor spotless whilst her stepmother and stepsisters lay abed.

Task complete—for now—Cynthia hurried to the scullery to begin the preparations for their breakfast. The sun was rising high, and the sleeping ladies usually awoke by noon. No two of them ever wanted the same dish, causing even more work in the kitchen to keep them from berating her or flinging the unwanted delicacies to the floor. Again.

Cynthia had never dreamt she should one day be an exhausted, bedraggled maid-of-all-work in her childhood home. As a young girl, she had never even wondered how their French chef created his masterful sauces and marvelous *pâte à choux*. She certainly hadn't imagined that after the death of her beloved, humble-born mother five years prior, Father would remarry a widowed lady with expensive tastes and two daughters of her own... Or that the following year, after Father's subsequent death, the three women would spend every penny of his life savings with breathtaking speed, until every servant had gone elsewhere and Cynthia was forced to become a scullion in her own home.

She would have left without hesitation if she had any money to her name—and if she could bear to abandon her parents' home and the remaining memory-imbued furnishings and keepsakes to the careless hands of her stepmother and stepsisters.

"Cynthia, you snail!" screamed a voice from the dining room. "Where are my eggs?"

That was Dorothea, the elder of Cynthia's two stepsisters and impossible to please—making her the darling of her mother. The screaming was often more to appease Lady Tremaine than to torture Cynthia, although it generated the same result. Had the eggs and kippers been ready five minutes earlier, Dorothea would have pronounced them "old" and "too cold" and sent Cynthia to begin all over again.

"Coming!" she called out as she hurried the heavy tray into the dining room.

Stasia was seated at the table as well, her pale face propped up by both hands, and her red curls awry. The sisters had spent the past night at a ball, and Stasia appeared the worse for wear. Perhaps the provided supper had not agreed with her.

Their mother, Lady Tremaine, appeared to still be abed.

A small blessing. As was the trio's absence from home the evening before. As much as Cynthia dreamed of attending a fancy ball one day, dressed like a princess, a few stolen hours of peace and quiet in which to catch up on her work and take a much-needed nap felt like a gift from the heavens.

She served generous portions onto the sisters' pre-warmed plates. "Here everything is, hot and fresh, as you like it."

Dorothea poked at her eggs with her fork, testing their consistency for some failing to report back to her mother—who always asked for the latest ways Cynthia had failed to live up to expectations.

Stasia simply groaned and dropped her face lower into her hands, ignoring the repast altogether.

Cynthia's stomach growled as she set the remaining dishes on the sideboard, though she knew better than to take a seat at the table.

Dorothea's black cat, Morningstar, darted out from beneath the sideboard.

"*Rowr*!" he screeched, clawing at Cynthia's slipper as he passed.

"Leave Morningstar alone!" Dorothea scolded Cynthia, despite her not having stepped anywhere near his paws or tail, scooping the demon feline onto her lap in order to feed him bits of her kippers.

"Please scream at her *quietly*," Stasia mumbled into her palms.

The sound of trumpets blaring at a distance startled Cynthia from arranging the dishes. "What was that?"

Dorothea rolled her eyes. "The royal parade."

"How dare they," Stasia moaned. "It's barely past noon."

"How dare who?" Cynthia asked, befuddled. "The Prince Regent?"

"Not Prinny, you featherwit. The visiting royalty from Italy. Prince Azzurro's hunt for an English bride is the only thing anyone has been talking about for months."

Cynthia was no featherwit. She had once boasted the finest tutors in London. It was not her fault that once the staff had been dismissed, there was no one left for Cynthia to chat with. Her only interaction with the outside world came from reading scraps of discarded newspapers and overhearing snippets of gossip between her stepmother and stepsisters.

"Come on, Stasia." Dorothea threw a bun at her sister. "We cannot miss him!"

"Cynthia didn't brush my hair," Stasia protested, lifting her face from her hands.

"Put on a bonnet," Dorothea snapped. "Or stay here with her, whilst the prince falls in love with *me*."

"Is he meant to select his bride this afternoon?" Cynthia asked.

"At tonight's grand ball, unless he falls in love beforehand." Dorothea dragged her sister out through the front door to the street, where a crowd was already forming.

Cynthia followed, careful to stay a few feet behind, lest the duo notice her presence and send her back into the kitchens.

Luckily, Dorothea and Stasia—like the rest of the gathering crowd—were too busy jostling each other and raising up on tiptoes to notice a scullery maid in a patched and tattered blue-and-brown dress lagging shyly behind.

Soldiers and musicians marched by first, followed by eight white stallions pulling an enormous, gilded open carriage. The crowd roared its approval at their first glimpse of the royal passengers. Several women shrieked in excitement. A few young ladies swooned at the sight of the Italian prince.

Even Cynthia's mouth fell open in awe.

"Who is *that?*" she blurted, slack-jawed and blushing.

"Prince Azzurro," a young woman to her right breathed dreamily. "He's come to select a bride from the best England has to offer. I hope he chooses me. Have you ever seen eyes so blue, hair so black, and shoulders so wide?"

"Not *him.*" Cynthia pointed as surreptitiously as she could. "There, seated *next* to him."

"That's his spinster sister, Princess Ammalia. She's here to help him find his match."

Dorothea spun about and caught Cynthia staring. "Don't think for a second that his royal highness will spare a glance for the likes of you. At that ball, either Stasia or I will win the hand of the prince. *You* won't even leave the scullery."

Cynthia couldn't care less about the prince.

Her eyes dazzled and her stomach filled with butterflies at the sight of the resplendent Princess Ammalia...

Whose black-lashed, bright blue gaze had just locked with Cynthia's.

CHAPTER 2

$\mathcal{T}$he horses, like Princess Ammalia's heart, came to a sudden stop.

She did not know what had impeded the progress of the royal stallions this time, but she did know exactly what had caused her own heart to fail, then to burst back into motion, beating twice as swiftly as before. She gazed out of the carriage in wonder.

Thousands of onlookers flooded the streets in the hopes of glimpsing visiting royalty. The teeming masses were what had clogged the escape path—er, parade route—the horses had been following. But it wasn't fear of a surging crowd that set Ammalia's blood pumping faster.

It was a woman.

She was toward the back of the throng, half-hidden from view. It didn't matter. She had the sort of ethereal beauty that could be *felt* from yards away and in the pitch black of night, if necessary.

It wasn't the golden blond hair or the plump

rose-petal pink lips that had caught Ammalia's eye. It wasn't even the high cheekbones or the becoming flush of color rising up her peaches-and-cream skin.

It was the wide blue eyes that had latched onto Ammalia's own, as if this woman, too, had felt the connection between them as strong as a thick metal chain capable of hauling a ship back to shore.

Anchored in place by eyes like those, Ammalia couldn't dream of going anywhere else. If the mass of jostling onlookers parted enough to let the horses trot anew, Ammalia would throw herself down from this carriage and elbow her way through the crowd until she reached—

"What are you looking at?" her brother Zurri asked with interest.

"Nothing," Ammalia said quickly.

But she could no more tear her enthralled eyes from this captivating woman than she could rip her pounding heart free from her chest.

Zurri followed the direction of his sister's gaze. "Who? Where?"

She didn't answer.

Their father, the king, was in the carriage behind theirs, no doubt watching his children closely. Not because he feared scandal—this entire spectacle was because the king loved to be the center of attention, at any cost. The bigger the drama, the better.

Nor did his majesty worry about the future of his only daughter, whom he'd given up caring about at the disappointing moment of her birth.

Neither Ammalia nor her theoretical children were of import. It was the male line that counted. Her brother was the future king. Rather than arrange a political alliance, Father was even allowing Zurri to select the most beautiful bride in all of England and align the two nations that way.

Ammalia, as the elder sibling and worthless female, was supposed to be finding this enviable match for her brother.

Zurri was, as always, the center of attention—just as he liked it. He needn't even be charming. Being a prince was more than enough for women everywhere to fall in love on sight.

"I don't care to know who's caught your eye," Zurri said petulantly, as though he were a child of six years, rather than a man of six-and-twenty. "I don't want anything or anyone that pleases *you*. You have terrible taste."

That was the rumor, anyway. Ammalia wouldn't have had to be the twenty-seven-year-old spinster sister, if she'd bothered to accept any of the many offers for her hand that cropped up repeatedly over the years, often from highly sought-after gentlemen.

Duke of this, Lord of that, His Royal Highness such-and-such. Ammalia was bored by them all, no matter how handsome and wealthy and well-connected they were. She didn't *like* men, and never had. Fortunately, as a royal princess, the one concession afforded her by her father was that she needn't marry any man against her will.

Of course, what Ammalia *willed* was to marry the woman of her dreams. This scenario was not a thing that existed—a publicly condoned Sapphic royal match wasn't even the stuff of fairy tales—but that hadn't stopped her from wanting it viscerally. She longed for love. To find a happy-ever-after with a woman who made her feel not unlike the one whose celestial gaze was still locked on Ammalia's.

Outside of her family, however, no one knew about her preferences. Although a princess could get away with almost anything, Father had warned her not to embroil the family in gossip or to draw attention away from her brother until after Zurri was safely wed, and the alliance with England secure.

Until then, Ammalia's wishes didn't come second—they didn't matter at all.

"All right, I give up," Zurri groused. "*Please* tell me who it is you cannot look away from."

Because her brother had said please, Ammalia gestured in the general direction of her mystery woman. Not too precisely, of course. With luck, one of the other screaming young ladies flanking her should catch Zurri's eye.

Unfortunately, Ammalia was not in luck.

"The one with the handkerchief tied to her head and the smudge of dirt on her face?" he asked in disbelief. "I suppose she'd be halfway passable, if she weren't dressed in rags."

To be honest, Ammalia hadn't noticed the smudge or the handkerchief or the patched and tattered gown. Even now, after Zurri had so uncharitably pointed it out, Ammalia could not make herself care about such inconsequential details.

She wanted to know all the things that *did* matter. Like, what was this woman's name? Was she spoken for? Did she like good wine and ocean sunsets and focaccia fresh from the oven and the smooth feel of cold mosaic tiles beneath one's bare feet on a warm summer's day? Would she like to experience all those things with Ammalia?

"Maybe your pauper is just the trick to add sparkle to my image," he mused thoughtfully. "A pet project, for the public's sake. Like the time I adopted that dog."

"*I* adopted the dog. You held that Pomeranian in your lap long enough to get your portrait painted, and then never gave the poor wretch another glance."

Zurri's stunt had generated the desired effect: young ladies all over the Parmenza region of Italy purchased penny copies of that portrait, and acquired Pomeranians of their own out of solidarity with the prince.

"It was furry," her brother protested. "I don't like things with fur. I might not mind—"

"No," Ammalia said firmly. "That woman is a person, not a Pomeranian. She's not to become your pet, even for a moment."

Zurri was not listening to her. His head was cocked to one side, his eyes narrowing with calculation. "She does have good bones, does she not? Perhaps with a bath and a better dress, she might become the English rose I've been looking for."

"No," Ammalia said again, the word coming out strangled.

Her relationship with Zurri was like this.

Though they loved each other, he and Ammalia had sniped and fought with each other for so long, they didn't know any other way to interact. If Zurri saw something his sister wanted, he took it from her. Ammalia didn't even *have* this woman, and already her brother was plotting how to take possession.

Interest from her brother could only spell disaster. For the poor young woman, who would either be leg-shackled to a spoilt brat—or publicly discarded by him in front of all her peers, with no more thought than he'd given the Pomeranian.

Ammalia wouldn't be able to gather the gorgeous woman up and take her home. Not after a public rejection by the prince. Instead, Ammalia would be forced to leave her behind...

Or else watch her become Parmenza's next princess and future queen. Living under the same roof, yet untouchable. For the rest of Ammalia's life.

THE PERKS OF LOVING A WALLFLOWER

PRIVATE ARC

THE PERKS OF LOVING A
WALLFLOWER

As a master of disguise, Thomasina Wynchester can be a polite young lady—or a bawdy old man. Anything to solve the case. Her latest assignment unveils a top-secret military cipher covering up an enigma that goes back centuries. But when Tommy's beautiful new client turns out to be the high-born lady she's secretly smitten with, more than her mission is at stake...

Bluestocking Miss Philippa York doesn't believe in love. Her cold heart didn't pitter-patter when she was betrothed to a duke, nor did it break when he married someone else. All Philippa desires is to rescue her priceless manuscript and decode its clues to unmask a villain. She hates that she needs a man's help—so she's delighted to discover the clever, charming baron at her side is in fact a woman. Her cold heart... did it just pitter-patter?

"Erica Ridley is a delight!"

—Julia Quinn

"A family of delightful scoundrels... I want to be a Wynchester!"
—Eloisa James

SNEAK PEEK

"*A*bsolutely not," Tommy said to Jacob and Marjorie the following afternoon at tea. She handed a baby hedgehog back to her brother. "Stop meddling."

"Is it difficult when you ask the pieman for a pie?" he pointed out reasonably. "Or when you give your direction to a hackney driver? We call those 'words.' Extremely adept practitioners can advance all the way to 'conversation.' You and Philippa should try it."

Marjorie refreshed the tea. "Tommy's never been in love with a hackney driver or a pieman."

"I've never been in love with any kind of man, no matter how delicious his pies," Tommy said. "I would no sooner fall in love with a man than I would the moon. And the moon is much prettier."

"But not as pretty as Philippa," her cursed siblings sang out.

If she held a pie, she'd toss it at them.

"I'm not enamored," she grumbled.

She was far past enamored. Tommy's romantic

thoughts had been filled with no one but Philippa almost from the first moment she saw her.

It might have stayed a passing infatuation if she and Chloe hadn't had to join the reading circle in the course of a prior mission to recover a stolen work of art. In the process, Chloe had fallen in love with conversing with fellow literature enthusiasts—as well as with Philippa's intended suitor.

And Tommy...had fallen for Philippa.

"When will Graham and Elizabeth return home?" Tommy asked in an unsubtle attempt to change the subject.

"Who knows?" Jacob turned over the baby hedgehog, which barely filled his palm. He rubbed its belly with a fingertip. The hedgehog responded by closing tight about his finger. "Graham is out gathering intelligence, and Elizabeth...is off shopping for rapiers."

Tommy should have joined her. Sword shopping had to be better than suffering through sibling matchmaking while attempting to enjoy an afternoon repast.

How Tommy missed Chloe! After Bean succumbed to smallpox last year, Tommy and Chloe had only grown closer. They'd spent months in a clandestine operation to liberate a stolen item from the Duke of Faircliffe.

And then Chloe married him.

Now she was the *Duchess of Faircliffe*. She wasn't here anymore to eat tea cakes and tickle baby hedgehogs. Her old bedchamber was still down the corridor from Tommy's, but nothing was left inside except unwanted furniture.

That was enough change for one year. Tommy's days were plenty full with missions and pies. She certainly didn't need to add "words" and "conversations" to her busy calendar.

Jacob produced an ornate snuffbox. "I cannot believe that our happy-go-lucky fearless adventuress is scared to talk to a *girl*."

"Woman," Marjorie corrected.

"You have the perfect excuse to approach Philippa." Jacob opened the snuffbox. It did not contain snuff. "We're helping her reading circle."

"I have no reason to talk to her," Tommy said. "The next meeting isn't for a week and we have no news yet anyway."

Jacob arched a brow. "So you'll just pine from afar in the meantime?"

"She's good at it," said Marjorie. "She's been practicing all year."

"Thank you, Marjorie," Tommy murmured.

The truth was, there was no use starting down a path that went nowhere. All good things ended. Especially when it came to people Tommy cared about. She had been orphaned at the age of four. Bean died. Chloe left. It was better to acknowledge relationships were temporary from the start than to get one's hopes and dreams and *feelings* tangled up in the matter.

Tommy was happy to infiltrate asylums and impersonate night watchmen. Resolving situations for clients was something she was good at.

The impossible situations in her own life, however, tended to stay impossible.

"What's the problem? There are no laws

against women sleeping with each other," Jacob pointed out.

"Maybe that is the problem," Marjorie said. "Tommy adores breaking laws."

"'Not illegal' isn't the same as 'accepted,' and you know it," Tommy said. "Graham is always deciphering messages in the advertisements. Why do you think the writer hid the true nature of that Sapphic country house party last month?"

"So men wouldn't attend," Marjorie said without hesitation.

"Probably," Jacob agreed.

Tommy ignored them. It had been an excellent party.

She was no stranger to desire and pleasure. Her lovers weren't looking for anything more than an evening's romp. Fun while it lasted. There was no expectation of gadding about town together in their *real* lives. Most didn't even share their true names.

It was perfectly fine. Tommy didn't need anything else. Or anyone else.

"Besides," she said, "there's no reason to believe Philippa would be interested in me even if I *were* to shower her with words and conversation. She's hunting for a husband. She almost married a duke. To people like the Yorks, rubbing shoulders with an untitled Wynchester—even platonically—is too scandalous to consider."

"She rubs shoulders with *Great-Aunt* Wynchester," Marjorie pointed out.

Tommy sent her a flat look. "Polite Society is not and will never be for me."

"Maybe Philippa doesn't want it either," Jacob suggested.

Tommy picked at her tea cake. "Maybe she does. We don't know. I'd rather never confess my feelings than to see her recoil in horror."

"What if she didn't recoil in horror?" Marjorie said softly.

"I still couldn't keep her," Tommy said. "Losing Philippa would be worse than never having her. If I lost the chance for friendship, I would be left with nothing."

"A simple conversation," Jacob insisted. "Not a sonnet about your admiration of her big brain and bigger bosom, but a regular, ordinary, words-and-ideas conversation about something other than the case. If you do that, I promise to stop hounding you."

Tommy glared at him.

"I promise, too," said Marjorie. "I'll even make the others promise as well. If you talk to Philippa for…fifteen minutes."

"Twenty," Jacob said quickly.

"Talk to Philippa for *twenty minutes?*" Tommy burst out. "About what?"

"Take her a kitten," Jacob suggested. "She likes Tiglet."

"Tiglet is a homing kitten," Tommy reminded him. "If she sets him down, he'll run back to Islington."

"Then you can give him back." Jacob tapped her on the nose. "See? He's a perennial conversation starter."

"I'm not giving her Tiglet," Tommy said firmly.

"You should hurry," said Marjorie. "Graham said she'll be traversing Hyde Park with her mother within the hour."

"Graham's not even here to be part of the conversation. He…" Tommy narrowed her eyes. "Did he plan this? Did *you* plan this? Am I under attack?"

"You're being manipulated into doing the thing you actually want to do," Jacob said cheerfully. "You cannot go to your grave without having tried at least once."

"I can't walk up to her as Tommy Wynchester. She doesn't *know* Tommy Wynchester, and besides, the daily promenade in Hyde Park is for the haut ton. Her mother wouldn't allow me twenty seconds, even if I were Lady Tommy. Mrs. York has been very clear that Philippa is only to fraternize with future suitors."

Jacob shrugged. "Then be one."

"Not a boatman," Marjorie said quickly. "Be someone Mrs. York would allow near her daughter."

A crafty smile spread on Jacob's face. "Be Baron Vanderbean."

"The new heir only exists on paper," Tommy reminded him.

Her brother raised his brows. "If no one's seen him, then no one can say you *aren't* him, can they?"

She supposed not.

The Baron Vanderbean who had rescued them all had held a minor peerage in his native Balcovia, a small principality in the Low Countries.

Although Bean had left generous trusts to each

of his adopted children, a society connection was one thing money could not purchase. Before he died, Bean had created a fictitious heir and heiress: Horace and Honoria Wynchester. By maintaining the sponsorship of the new Baron Vanderbean and the chaperonage of his highborn sister, the Wynchester orphans could still enjoy access to places and people that would have snubbed them if they had no titled connection.

Ironic that an imaginary lord held more power than a real woman.

"You want me to be Baron Vanderbean," Tommy repeated.

Just saying the words sent gooseflesh over her skin. Baron Vanderbean was *Bean*.

Bean was dead.

Tommy would do anything to have her father back. She wanted nothing to do with a made-up relative. And she couldn't imagine taking over Bean's name. If she pretended to be his "son," Horace Wynchester, everyone would call her Baron Vanderbean. She wasn't certain she could handle it.

But she also didn't want her family to see her hesitant and meek. Tommy was the one who *did* things. She could be anyone. She just wasn't sure she could do…this.

"It's a bad idea," she said. There. *She* wasn't weak. The *plan* was defective.

"Why?" Jacob asked.

"For one," she replied slowly, "if I play Baron Vanderbean, no one else can do it."

Jacob smirked. "Who else was going to do it?"

Well, fair enough.

Marjorie and Elizabeth were dreadful at playing men, and Jacob's dark brown skin made it unlikely for him to be Bean's son by blood. Graham's golden bronze coloring might let him get away with it, but his temperament never would.

Tall, thin, white, curve-less Tommy was the most believable as Bean's male heir.

That wasn't all. She could have more honest interactions with Philippa as a gentleman, rather than dressed as an old lady at her reading circle. Tommy rubbed the back of her neck nervously. *Could* she do it?

"Besides," Jacob said. "The new heir has served his usefulness."

Marjorie picked up a tea cake. "Baron Vanderbean *was* our entrée into society, but now Chloe provides that function. The approval of the Duke and Duchess of Faircliffe carries far more weight than ties to a reclusive foreign lord."

Jacob stopped playing with his hedgehog. "Think about it, Tommy. The baron identity was for any Wynchester who needed it, however we needed it. And the person who needs it is you."

"And maybe Philippa," Marjorie added.

Tommy set down her tea. "Twenty minutes of conversation as Baron Vanderbean, and you'll never mention my tendre for Philippa again?"

Jacob and Marjorie touched their hands to their hearts and lifted their fingers to the sky. The Wynchester salute was how the siblings swore their vows. Both their faces were innocent.

Tommy narrowed her eyes at them.

"Twenty complete minutes," Jacob said. "Of actual words. Not twenty minutes of pining in close proximity."

"It's a promenade," Tommy reminded him. "I'll be lucky to speak to her for *ten* minutes."

Jacob smiled. "Then you'll have to do it twice."

THANK YOU

AND SNEAK PEEKS

THANK YOU FOR READING

Love talking books with fellow readers?

Join the *Historical Romance Book Club* for prizes, books, and live chats with your favorite romance authors:
   Facebook.com/groups/HistRomBookClub

Check out the **Patreon** for bonus content, sneak peeks, advance review copies and more:
   https://www.patreon.com/EricaRidleyFans

And don't miss the **official website**:
   www.EricaRidley.com/books

ABOUT THE AUTHOR

Erica Ridley is a *New York Times* and *USA Today* best-selling author of witty, feel-good historical romance novels, including THE DUKE HEIST, featuring the Wild Wynchesters. Why seduce a duke the normal way, when you can accidentally kidnap one in an elaborately planned heist?

In the *12 Dukes of Christmas* series, enjoy witty, heartwarming Regency romps nestled in a picturesque snow-covered village. After all, nothing heats up a winter night quite like finding oneself in the arms of a duke!

Two popular series, the *Dukes of War* and *Rogues to Riches*, feature roguish peers and dashing war heroes who find love amongst the splendor and madness of Regency England.

When not reading or writing romances, Erica can be found eating couscous in Morocco, ziplining through rainforests in Central America, or getting hopelessly lost in the middle of Budapest.

～

Let's be friends! Find Erica on:
www.EricaRidley.com